Anthony Burgess

# ONE HAND CLAPPING

VINTAGE

Published by Vintage 1996

2 4 6 8 10 9 7 5 3 1

First published in Great Britain by
Peter Davies Ltd, 1961

Vintage
Random House, 20 Vauxhall Bridge Road,
London SW1V 2SA

Random House Australia (Pty) Limited
20 Alfred Street, Milsons Point, Sydney
New South Wales 2061, Australia

Random House New Zealand Limited
18 Poland Road, Glenfield,
Auckland 10, New Zealand

Random House South Africa (Pty) Limited
PO Box 2263, Rosebank 2121, South Africa

Random House UK Limited Reg. No. 954009

A CIP catalogue record for this book
is available from the British Library

ISBN 0 09 959081 6

Papers used by Random House UK Ltd are natural,
recyclable products made from wood grown in sustain-
able forests. The manufacturing processes conform to
the environmental regulations of the country of origin

Typeset in 10½/12 Sabon by
Palimpsest Book Production Limited,
Polmont, Stirlingshire
Printed and bound in Great Britain by
Cox & Wyman, Reading, Berkshire

# ONE HAND CLAPPING

Born in Manchester in 1917, Anthony Burgess was educated at the Xaverian College in the city and at Manchester University, of which he held a doctorate. He served in the army from 1940 to 1956, and as a colonial education officer in Malaya and Borneo from 1954 to 1960, in which year, as he put it, 'his brief but irreversible unemployability having been decreed by a medical death sentence, he decided to try to live by writing'. His output comprises over fifty books. He was a Visiting Fellow of Princeton University and a Distinguished Professor of City College, New York. He was created a Commandeur des Arts et des Lettres by the French President and a Commandeur de Merite Culturel by Prince Rainier of Monaco. Anthony Burgess died in 1993.

# BY ANTHONY BURGESS

## Novels

The Long Day Wanes:
  Time For A Tiger
  The Enemy In The Blanket
  Beds In The East
The Right To An Answer
The Doctor Is Sick
The Worm And The Ring
Devil Of A State
One Hand Clapping
A Clockwork Orange
The Wanting Seed
Honey For The Bears
Inside Mr Enderby
Nothing Like The Sun: A Story of
  Shakespeare's Love-Life
The Eve Of Saint Venus
A Vision Of Battlements
Tremor Of Intent
Enderby Outside
M F
Napoleon Symphony
The Clockwork Testament; Or,
  Enderby's End
Beard's Roman Woman
Abba Abba
Man Of Nazareth
1985
Earthly Powers
The End Of The World News
Enderby's Dark Lady
The Kingdom Of The Wicked
The Pianoplayers
Any Old Iron
The Devil's Mode (short stories)
A Dead Man In Deptford
Byrne
Cyrano de Bergerac

## Autobiography

Little Wilson And Big Good
You've Had Your Time

## For Children

A Long Trip To Teatime
The Land Where The Icecream
  Grows

## Theatre

Oberon Old And New
Blooms Of Dublin

## Verse

Moses

## Non-Fiction

English Literature: A Survey For
  Students
They Wrote In English
  (for Italian schools)
Language Made Plain
Here Comes Everybody: An
  Introduction To James Joyce
  For The Ordinary Reader
The Novel Now: A Student's
  Guide To Contemporary Fiction
Urgent Copy: Literary Studies
Shakespeare
Joysprick: An Introduction To The
  Language Of James Joyce
New York
Hemingway And His World
On Going To Bed
This Man And Music
Homage to Quert Yuiop
Mozart And The Wolf Gang
A Mouthful Of Air

## Translations

The New Aristocrats
The Olive Trees Of Justice
The Man Who Robbed Poor Boxes
Cyrano de Bergerac
Oedipus The King

## Editor

A Shorter Finnegans Wake

TO HAZEL

# I

I WAS JANET Shirley, *née* Barnes, and my husband was
Howard Shirley, and in this story he was nearly twenty-seven
and I was just gone twenty-three. We lived on the Shortshawe
Council Estate in North Bradcaster, Number 4 Cranmer
Road off Whitgift Road which leads into town, and we paid
thirty-two and six a week rent. Just up the road from us was,
and is, I guess, Shoe Lane which was on the TV commercials
as Shining Shoe Lane, which made all those who lived there
very boastful in a silly way, as if they'd done something clever.
All the roads on our side were named after bishops – Ridley
Road, Latimer Road, Fisher Road and Laud Road – and there
was never any call to use those in TV commercials. Howard
worked at the Oak Crescent Used Car Mart and I helped to
fill up the shelves at the Hastings Road Supermarket, so at
the time there was nothing very special about us. We had a
TV, a radio with a strap like a handbag for carrying round
the house, a washing-machine, a vac, but no car of our own or
children. We had been married since I was nineteen. That was
not young in my family, my mother was married at sixteen and
my sister Myrtle (Sadler) at seventeen. My sister Myrtle, as
you'll see, made a mess of her marriage, but that was nothing
to do with marrying young, she would have made a mess at
whatever age, marrying a man like Michael.

Howard and I met when I was still at the Hawthorn Road
Secondary Modern School, only fifteen, and he had been out
of the Grammar School three years. I looked older than I was,
like most of the girls did, and as there wasn't a lot to learn
in school we used to spend a lot of time on our appearance.
I will say, though, that Miss Spenser took us twice a week

1

for Make-up, Deportment and Dress Sense, but the poor old thing did not know much about it. Besides, it always seemed wrong to us girls to have something like that in a school, and that the tax-payer's money should be spent better. There was also Ballroom Dancing and what was called Homecraft. None of the teachers knew very much about what they taught and it was pathetic, sometimes, the way they tried to make our schooldays happy. There was young Mr Slessor with the beard who said he was a beatnik and called us cats and chicks. He was supposed to teach English but said like he didn't dig the king's jive. Crazy, man, real cool. It was pathetic. Mr Thornton, who taught history, said he knew we wouldn't be interested in all those old kings and queens so he just played his guitar and sang very dull songs, so we weren't allowed to have any history and I was good at that at the primary. Then there was old puffing and blowing Mr Portman, a portly man you could say, who took us for General Science, but he was a bit too fond of asking us girls to go round and help him in the little apparatus room, breathing hard on us. I hit him once but he never did anything about that. I came out of Hawthorn Road Secondary Mod knowing nothing, but they always say that if you're a girl, and pretty like I was, you didn't need to know all that much. I could look smashing, though I say it myself, and I got whistled at, and I could do snappy back-answers, like when some boy said at a dance, 'What's cooking, good-looking?' you had to reply, 'Nothing spectacular, Dracula.' But sometimes they were so ignorant they didn't know what Dracula was, so you had to think of something else.

Howard wasn't like that, he was a serious boy and good at athletics. He was modest, really, despite being smashing-looking in a very dark way, and he used to say he hadn't the brains for the better class of jobs (which are not well-paid, anyway) and was better at practical things like car-engines than books and figures and the rest of the things that boys go in for when they've got G.C.E. Ordinary Level. Howard did very well in his G.C.E., but there was some trouble about his papers, because the examiners said he'd cribbed, just copying word for word from the books. But it was explained by his headmaster that Howard had one of those very unusual brains like a camera, it could sort of photograph things. It was really uncanny sometimes, the way his brain worked. You could give Howard anything to look at, as it might be a song or a page of a book or a list of names or anything like that, and he'd look at it then close his eyes and then speak out without making any mistakes what he'd read. He should really have been on the TV with it, which he was in a way later, as you'll see, but he always said it didn't mean cleverness or anything like that. It was only a photographic brain, he called it, and he said that a lot of people had it and it meant nothing at all.

We met because we were both keen on dancing, doing rock 'n' roll in a very athletic way, Howard throwing me over his shoulder and me doing the splits to loud applause, and all that sort of thing, so that we won one or two prizes and even went in for some of the big competitions, though at those we always seemed to get beaten by couples on holiday from Denmark or Sweden, very blonde and slim and sunburned all over. I was very blonde and slim too, but not in that sort of way, more in an English way, if you see what I mean, like some of the models on the TV commercials. I've always looked older than my years, and I never seemed to go through a real teenage stage, with pop-singer clubs and screaming and all that. I think that's what appealed to Howard, not that I've ever been really *serious*, but I had a bit more sense than the others.

Howard didn't say he loved me till about six months after we first met, and even then I used to go out with other boys – the local talent, I used to call it, but there wasn't much of it really – but none of them was quite like Howard. Howard would look up at the moon and the stars and say, 'Think of them being all those millions of miles away,' and sometimes he'd give you the exact figures which his brain had taken a snapshot of. Howard had a deep voice and he could make it sound like Michael Denison. He could have been very good at selling things, that voice being a big help, but he never had much ambition. It was me who mentioned marriage first – I was sixteen at the time – but he said we'd have to wait. I said to Howard that he'd have to do better than just working at the Elm Street Garage, getting all oily and greasy, but he said the money was all right. We quarrelled on and off about him having no ambition and we parted for a whole three months, me going round with one boy after another, and none of them much good with their off-beat finger-snapping to the music and their talk about getting the message and man, that sends me. It was like Mr Slessor at school all over again. I used to see Howard glooming about the town, all on his own, and when he started drinking (which I heard about) we had to make it up. Then, just after my seventeenth birthday, we got engaged. After that, we got down to seriously making plans and saving up, and Howard got this better job at the Oak Crescent Used Car Mart. We started making love more seriously than before, but I wouldn't let it get too serious, though time and again I was on the point of giving myself to him in the park, what we call the Clough, among the trees. Anyway, to cut a long story short, we got married when I was nineteen. It was a nice little white wedding at St Olave's with a reception afterwards at Horrocks's, port and sherry and a three-tiered cake from Renshaw's, and there we were kissing everybody and being kissed. This reception set my father back a bit, but he was earning good money at Baxendale's (foreman) and when his two daughters first came into the world he must have known he'd have all that expense sooner or later. Anyway, there we were, Howard and me, man and wife, let no man put asunder.

We had our name down for a council house, living in the meantime with my mother and father (Howard was a blitz orphan but brought up by his aunt in Tinmarsh). We didn't care for this sharing very much and the walls were very thin. We were lucky, though, because there wasn't too big a waiting-list in Bradcaster, and it was a real thrill to get into our very own home with our own few sticks of furniture which we kept adding to. That's always a real pleasure, buying things for the home, and our presents to each other for a long time were coal-scuttles and kitchen-sets and things like that. We had a lot of things on the H.P., like most people, but Howard had a good clean job with basic wage and commission, and there I was helping to fill up the shelves at the Hastings Road

Supermarket with baked beans and soapflakes. Whether we wanted children or not we couldn't make up our minds about, and Howard was always talking very seriously about the Threat of Another War and the Hydrogen Bomb and it not being fair to any child to bring it into the world these days. He got more and more serious when we were married and talked a lot about what he called his Responsibilities. I didn't take too much notice of what Howard said, but I couldn't make up my mind whether I wanted to be a mother or not. Sometimes in the evening when we sat looking at the TV, Howard in the fireside chair and me on the rug beside him, the feeling would come over me that it would be nice to have a little child upstairs calling down, 'Mummy.' This was especially during the commercials, showing mother and daughter both protected by the same soap, or the mother loving her children so much that she washed all their clothes in Blink or whatever it was (they're all the same, really) or the mother and father and little children sitting down to a good nourishing dinner of Somebody-or-other's fish fingers. But Howard and I had a good time together, dancing in the evenings or going to the flicks (which is only like a bigger kind of more uncomfortable TV which you have to pay for), even though it wasn't what you would call an exciting sort of life. At week-ends sometimes Howard would borrow one of the cars from the Car Mart and we would go off into the country and have tea somewhere. Once or twice he borrowed a really big car – a Bentley, or Cadillac, or something, I don't know much about cars – and then we'd go to dinner at one of these hotels in one of the country towns miles away from Bradcaster, one of those places all low ceilings and brass on the walls and a smell of Oxo gravy everywhere, and for all anybody knew, me glamorous and Howard with his BBC voice and the big car outside, we could be somebody really big. We played it real cool, as poor Mr Slessor would say. That was nice now and again.

I could see that Howard fretted sometimes. As I said, he wasn't ambitious, but he said, once or twice, especially after some film or TV programme or something he'd read in the *Daily Window*, 'Oh, what will we ever see of the world?'

or 'You ought to be dripping with real diamonds and be all wrapped up in mink.'

'Well,' I'd say, 'why don't you do something about it?' – not meaning that really, of course, because we really had a lot to be thankful for, what with a home and a TV and a bottle of port in the cupboard and bitter lemons in the pantry and able to go out now and again and live it up in a modest sort of way.

One night Howard said, very seriously, 'I'd never steal money, not because it's not right to steal, which it's not, but because it makes everything too easy. I mean, we're a bit old-fashioned where I work, and we just stuff cash into this very old-fashioned till, and sometimes it's quite big sums. I could nick a couple of hundred just like that, then the two of us on the train to London or somewhere, and they'd never catch us. But it's not worth it. If we're to get money we're to get it honestly. If we ever get it at all we'll get it by luck, not by what you or I could do. Because what are we, really?'

'Thanks very much,' I said in my sarky tone.

'No, no,' he said, frowning. 'You know what I mean. We don't have much to give to the world, talent or anything like that, I mean. We haven't got very much of anything that the world would fall over itself to want to buy. Besides, what I'd want for you is the real big money, the money so big you'd be able to light cigarettes with it.'

'You push on with the pools, my lad,' I said. 'Somebody's got to win.' We were doing Number 42 Litplan at the time.

'Oh, s – t on the pools,' Howard said, cross, and I was cross back, not liking that kind of language. The man at school who'd taught maths had gone in for that sort of language, thinking it made him popular with the boys. Mr Lithgow. 'What I mean is,' said Howard, 'is I'd like to live like a millionaire for, say, one month.'

'And then come back to the Used Car Mart?'

'No,' said Howard. He was always full of surprises.

'Then to snuff it, having tasted a bit of life. Because, when all's said and done, there's not all that much to live for, is there?'

'Thanks very much,' I said again.

'Yes, yes, I've got you to live for, and if I went off I'd want to have the two of us going off together, one flesh like it said in the marriage vows. Sometimes,' he said dreamily, 'when I'm at work and waiting for customers I think about the two of us living like kings and not bothering about the future. Because there may not be any future to bother about, you know. Not for anybody, one of these days. And it's a wicked world.'

'It's not the world that's wicked,' I said. 'It's the people that's in it.' I had on the floor a 1s. 7d. box of Toffs, and I bulged out my cheek with one of these in it. Then, for some reason, and I'll never understand men, he smiled and was down on the rug hugging and kissing me, saying, 'Oh, you're marvellous.'

After a bit he said, 'It was just a thought, that's all. It's a question of your mood, I suppose, and how you're feeling.' I frowned at that, not understanding how that fitted in with anything, and then I said, looking at the ormolu clock we had bought very cheap, it being on the mantelpiece:

'It's time for *Over and Over*. Nearly, anyway.'

'What's that?' he said, getting up from the floor.

'Oh, I'd forgotten.' This was the first Thursday evening that Howard had been home for a long time, him having been in the habit of going to see his auntie at Tinmarsh, her living alone now with him married, and also not very well. But she was now in hospital at Rosscourt and that was much too far away for visiting. 'Oh,' I said, 'it's this quiz-show and it's this boy who's up for the thousand-pound question. On horse-racing it is.'

'That's a queer sort of thing for a boy to know anything about. Is he a stable-boy?'

'No, secondary mod like I was. The way I look at it, a young lad's got to fill his mind with something these days. That stands to reason, there not being much taught at school if my school was anything to go by.'

Howard switched on and then the set warmed up and then you could hear the voices whispering and then booming and then you could see the picture. It's always a bit of a thrill, that, when the voices start coming up, and it's always a bit of a shock and a surprise when you can see the picture. Like

7

a miracle. This picture showed a very plump blonde singer and a very silly comedian. 'Oh, Christ,' said Howard, 'look at that. The wonders of modern science and the pleasures of bloody civilisation. God help the blasted lot of us.' He was in a real swearing mood this evening but I didn't say anything more because he was sweet as well.

'That'll be over in five minutes,' I said. The singer and the comedian were doing a kind of final number in night clothes, with a big cardboard moon up above, and she was wearing a toreador jama, very snazzy. Then they finished with a close-up of their back teeth on the last note, and we had the commercials. Fivepence off fish-cakes and threepence off Giant Size Splazz. Wait a bit longer and they'll give them away. And *our* washing-machine, two pound ten cheaper than when we bought it. Cheek. Then this quiz-show started. Howard watched it with interest. The quiz-master was a sort of American or Irishman, you couldn't be sure which, with a very pointy sort of face. A lot of rather ugly and silly people came on and were asked easy questions about things, the quiz-master being very good at helping them, a bit too much so, I thought. The studio audience went mad clapping when one stupid middle-aged couple got the right answer when the quiz-master said, 'Fill in the blank here. Salt, mustard, vinegar –' The couple looked at him, blank, so he said it again. 'Salt, mustard, vinegar –' Then the man of the couple said, 'H.P. Sauce.' 'No advertising, please,' said the quiz-master, which was silly, because the whole of ITV is advertising. Then he said, 'If I gave you pen, ink and *pepper*, perhaps you could write it down.' And the woman of the couple said, 'I thought as how we got to say it.' Then the quiz-master said, 'It's in a pot, see. In the cruet. Ah-choo. Ah-choo. AH-CHOO.' Then they got it and were so pleased at getting it, and so was the studio audience, that you'd think it was some really big deal. So they got eight pounds but wouldn't risk going on to sixteen, and I couldn't say that I blamed them. 'Dead stupid,' said Howard. 'Where do they get these people from?'

'They get put on a waiting-list,' I said, 'like for council houses.'

'Well,' said Howard, 'I never did.' That's just an expression.

8

After the interval and more advertisements, this little boy came on for the thousand-pound question, a round-faced young lad with no tie on, though it was the depths of autumn. He spoke in a gobbly sort of voice, very nervous, just like any young lad will speak, and the quiz-master told him not to be like that. So then they put him in a box with a clock with a big second-hand right behind him, and the quiz-master was shaking more nervously than the lad as he got the paper with the questions on. This lad put on his earphones and said he was ready, and the quiz-master said:

'There are three parts to this question. You've got to give the names of the winner, owner, trainer and jockey for each of three races in particular years. Have you got that?' The lad had got it. You could see the quiz-master was very anxious for the lad to win, because he knew they'd all shout 'Shame' if he didn't and make out it was all his, the quiz-master's, fault. So then he said, 'Number one. Think carefully before you answer. You have thirty seconds. The Two Thousand Guineas, 1935.' Quick as a flash the lad said:

'Bahram. The Aga Khan. F. Butters and F. Fox.' And then he said, which wasn't asked for, 'Seven to two.'

The quiz-master went mad and the audience went mad about that being the right answer. Then he asked, 'The Oaks, 1957.' The lad said:

'Easy. Carrozza. Her Majesty the Queen. Murlett. Lester Piggott up. I think it was a hundred to eight.' More going mad because it was right and then there was a terrible deathly hush, because if the lad got this last one wrong, even a bit of it, all his knowing about the odds in the other races wouldn't do him one little scrap of good. So here came the last one, and even Howard was leaning forward with his mouth open. 'Winner, owner, trainer, jockey. The Derby, 1899.' And this lad, with no trouble at all, blurted it straight out:

'Flying Fox. Duke of Westminster, J. Porter, M. Cannon.' But he said he couldn't remember the odds.

'Never mind the odds, boy,' shouted the quiz-master. 'You've won yourself a thousand pounds.' And then this young lad was dragged out of the box and everybody was yelling and screaming and the girl came on to give him his cheque and kissed him and the lad blushed and you could see he didn't like being given a cheque, he'd expected to have it all in real money. Howard switched off and all the yelling and cheering went out like a light. 'Well,' he said, 'it still seems all wrong that a young boy like that should have his head stuffed full of horse-racing while he's still at school. A lot of useless rubbish, that's what it is.'

'Not so useless,' I chipped in. 'He got a thousand quid out of it, didn't he?'

'Yes, he did, I suppose, but it isn't right for a young boy. An adult's different, of course. An adult doesn't have homework and so on. A thousand quid,' said Howard.

'You could have a go if you wanted to,' I said. 'You've always said that you've got just that kind of brain.'

'I'd never get near it,' said Howard. 'It stands to reason it must be a fiddle.'

'Why does it?'

'It just does, that's all.' There were times when Howard could be very unreasonable. Once he'd got an idea in his skull you couldn't get it out, even though it must have been obvious to him that he was being unreasonable. So I went to get the supper, which was baked beans on toast tonight. You'd think I'd be fed up with baked beans, seeing them all day long in the Supermarket. But they're an easy dish to put, and there's a fair amount of nourishment in them. I liked to keep Howard well fed. He could be very sweet at times.

# 2

THAT THAT I'VE already written and you've read is not really part of the story. The story begins about now, so now I'm gone twenty-three and Howard's nearly twenty-seven in this story, and you can imagine us both being a bit older than in that last bit where we were on the rug. We didn't change much really and our life went on much the same, except that Howard liked to read more and sometimes swore at the *Daily Window*, which he said was a rag. But we still went on taking it. And we still went on watching the TV. And we had the same jobs as we had before.

One morning, and it was a miserable autumn morning outside in the street, I was in the Hastings Road Supermarket filling up the shelves as usual, singing to myself. It was cosy being there with the other girls, wearing the RAF blue overalls and doing this nice easy work while the shoppers went round with their wire baskets and the reckoning machines on the tills went rattling away, and the place was brightly coloured with the packets and tins of things. And there was a smell of cheese and bacon, very faint, mixed with the stuff they sprayed all round the place to keep it sweet. But Howard, who had some awful expressions, said it smelled like a whore's bedroom. Not that he really knew what such smelled like, him having been a pretty good boy all round, even on his national service. And he didn't come into the Supermarket all that much, either, usually preferring to meet me outside to take me home at the end of the day.

Now, who should come in this morning but my sister Myrtle, looking for me. She was in a terrible state. She was three years older than me and she had this sherry-coloured

11

hair, copied from the heiress Bobo Sigrist, done in a bingle.
Manzanilla was the colour the hairdresser called the sherry-
colour Myrtle had. But she looked ill and terrible. she said:

'Oh, there you are. Look, I can't stand it any longer. I won't
stay in that house one day more with him. Please let me come
and stay with you for a bit.'

'It's Michael, is it?' I said. 'What's he been up to now?'

'Oh,' she said, 'it's not the drinking I mind, nor his swearing
either. Last night he tried to beat me. And this morning
he tried to have a crack at me before he went out.' Her
husband, Michael Sadler, worked in some shop where they
sold typewriters and what were called office accessories. A
very moody sort of a man, but handsome and knowing it.

'What does he want to beat you for?'

'He says he can't stand the sight of me nor the sound of
my voice.' Now Myrtle was a pretty girl, though less perhaps
than me, though of course her marriage had worn her down
and made her mouth droopy and given her bags under the
eyes. But I could understand that about the voice. Myrtle
had one of these scratchy high voices, always going nya
nya nya nya nya, and I could see that anybody might get
fed up living with that, but it seemed no excuse for beating
her up.

'Where did he beat you? Show me.'

We were in a sort of bay, all tins of soup, mostly cut-
price mulligatawny, and there was nobody about, but Myrtle
looked prim both ways, as if she was going to cross the road,
then she turned round and lifted the bottom of her jumper and
showed me her back. You could see the marks of fingers there
in a kind of fingery bruise, all blue and brown.

'That's a beauty,' I said. But I wasn't satisfied with her
reasons. I felt sure there was something more in it than just
her face and her voice. I said, 'I don't think you're telling me
the truth. Not the whole truth.' That was like a court scene
on the TV. I knew Myrtle, you see. I knew that Myrtle must
have been up to something. Not that I altogether blamed her,
knowing Michael. Michael had as good as driven her more
than once into the arms of another man. It was a terrible
marriage they had.

Myrtle pouted a bit. She had on this Golden Frost lipstick. 'Well,' she said, 'he reckoned I'd been carrying on with Charlie Evans.'

'And you have been, haven't you?'

'Well, there was nothing in it. And, anyway, there was Michael carrying on himself, wasn't there? And getting drunk on top of it. *And* swearing.' She sniffed in a sort of ladylike way. We never liked swearing much in our family.

'Well, what do you want to do?' I asked.

'Teach him a lesson,' said Myrtle. 'Let him fetch and carry for himself for a bit. And I'm not getting a wink of sleep neither. Let him try getting rid of his nasty temper on the kitchen stove, say. I want to come and stay in your spare room for a bit. But he mustn't know, see. Get him worried. Besides, I'm not going to let myself be bashed about like that.'

'You could go and stay with Mum and Pop for a bit, couldn't you?'

'Do me a favour. With her going on about I told you so and all that jazz?' Myrtle had some of these expressions, having been to our school also. 'Gloating about me making a mess of things and she never liked Michael anyway and all that jazz.' She repeated herself a lot. 'Bring him to his senses, that's all. Get him worried. Besides –' Then she was on again about not letting herself get bashed. Poor Myrtle. She never did have much sense. I think she really thought she was so attractive and Michael loved her so much really that he'd break his heart with her being away and would go mad like a quiz audience when she came back to him again. Anyway, I said:

'All right, bring your things along at dinner-time.' What we did at dinner-time was to go home and have a cooked dinner, something I'd left in the oven like a casserole or a bacon-and-egg pie. I knocked off at twelve-thirty and Howard at one o'clock, so the table was laid when he got in at ten-past and as his boss used to let him drive himself home in one of the used cars with an advertisement on it he was able to drive me back to the Supermarket at about twenty to two, this being a bit late but nobody saying anything about it. Then Howard would go back to our house and do the washing-up, then be ready to go back to the Used Car Mart at two o'clock. In the evening we'd have tea – pie and cake and jam – and later on, as you've seen, we'd have something fried like bacon and egg or sausages or something like baked beans on toast. At least, you've seen me getting supper ready and it was baked beans. At the end of the day for both of us, both places closing at six, Howard would walk round fairly quickly to the Supermarket and I'd have time to have made up and put my coat on before we walked back, if it was a fine evening, or else took the bus. It wasn't very far. Oak Crescent was off Yew Tree Road and that was off Whitgift Road, at the other side of Whitgift Road were all these roads with the names of historic battles, of which Hastings Road was one. Then you passed Waterloo Street with Naseby Crescent leading off it, then the bishops started and we were the third of these bishops. Anyway, I said:

'All right, bring your things along at dinner-time.'

'Bless you, kid,' she said. 'Just for a few days. And I've not been sleeping very well, either.'

I didn't see how she thought she'd be able to sleep any better at our house than in her own flat, which was the other side of town, because Howard could be very noisy at night and very likely to be heard all over the house, not so much snoring as groaning in his sleep and shouting things out. Sometimes also he would walk in his sleep and I did not dare to wake him up, that being dangerous. Anyway, she'd see for herself, wouldn't she? Not that Howard really disturbed me all that much, as I was used to him.

Well, anyway, Myrtle came along with her things and I'd fixed up the spare bedroom (what we called, in joke of course, the Nursery) for her and we'd set the table and Myrtle had made herself look very smart with more of this Golden Frost lipstick by the time Howard got in. He looked a bit surprised to see Myrtle there, but she simpered at him and made a bit with the eyelashes, so he just grunted. Myrtle would not have minded making a bit of a dead set at my Howard, but Howard was still very serious and I, though I say it myself, was the only woman for him. Myrtle tried to make it very clear to both of us, but to Howard especially, that if her husband Michael came round looking for her we were to say she was not there and that we didn't have any idea of her whereabouts. Howard said:

'Lies, you see. Life's all telling lies nowadays. All cheating and being a stranger to the truth. It's what those horses of Dean Swift say, that you've got a tongue in your head in order to tell people things to their advantage and not to deceive them. That what language is for is communication.' And he went on a bit longer about these talking horses, so that Myrtle looked at him as if he was a nut-case. I could see myself that Howard was thinking of some cowboy programme or other for kids, Dean Swift perhaps being in it. He liked to watch these kids' films in a kind of gloomy sort of way on Thursday afternoons while I was getting ready our special half-day-off tea, Thursday being early closing day in Bradcaster. Myrtle said:

'I don't call it really lies, saying that I'm not in when Michael calls. *If* he calls, that is, though I think he's bound to. If it is lies it's only what they call white lies.'

'Look,' said Howard, looking very smashing and fierce and putting down his knife and fork, for we were eating cheese-and-onion pie, plenty for three. 'I don't like lies and I don't like cheating, no matter how small it is. Now I've had a row this morning with old Watts who's my boss about cheating. Now I come home for my dinner and I find proposals for cheating put forward in my house by my own sister-in-law.'

'Oh,' said Myrtle, and you could see she was ready to do the old serviette-throwing-down act and get up and run upstairs snivelling. So I said to Howard:

'Why, what was it all about, Howard?' Howard said:

'Oh, it was with a Yankee car, about mixing oil and sawdust into the gearbox so that you can't hear the sound of the gears being worn. He's been talking to somebody somewhere, you could see that.' And then Howard went on about dirty tricks being played in the used car business. Old Watts his boss had talked about painting the tyres to make the treads look a lot better than they were, and then Howard had insisted that some customer or other should try out the

15

second-hand car he thought of buying on a good stretch of road, anything under ten miles, according to Howard, being no good. Moreover, Howard said that you should drive also on a rough stretch because that tested the steering and you could hear the rattles and squeaks better that way. And he said it was up to a customer to check the oil pressure, because if the oil pressure got low when the car heated up to normal that meant something had to be done about the rings and the valves or something, and if there was smoke that meant the car was using oil. And if there was too much oil on the outside that meant a cracked block, and it also meant a cracked block if the stick came out with a lot of gravy in the oil, because there was water in there. And the customer ought to check the transmission and the rear end for grease leaks and cracks, and so he went on and on, so that Myrtle just stared at him. Then Myrtle said:

'But I thought you sold cars, not bought them.'

'Buy them and sell them,' said Howard, 'and try to be fair to the buyers and the sellers. I hate cheating, as I've said, and I won't cheat for old Watts or anybody like him, and if old Watts doesn't care for that approach to the bloody work, well, he knows what he can do with his job.'

Anyway, he said no more about letting on to Michael that his wife was staying in our house, so the rest of our dinner was fairly peaceful. Myrtle said she'd do the washing-up and have a bit of tea ready for us when we came in if we liked. So I said it was a smashing idea and I'd leave it to her. I envied her really, having the nice cosy house all to herself all afternoon, a nice read by the fire of my woman's paper and then Music While You Work at 3.45 and then Mrs Dale at 4.30. A nice life for any woman, and one that Myrtle had had ever since she got married and didn't really appreciate. There's nothing like a winter's afternoon when you're all dozy and have got nothing to do, just sitting by the fire and dreaming a bit, romancing about who you might have married instead of the one you did, seeing yourself in dark glasses and a playsuit in Bermuda or somewhere and a handsome rogue with white teeth and a bronzed Tarzan torso leaning over you with a cigarette-lighter and you giving him a sort of mysterious look as you take the light, though of course you've got your sunglasses on and he can't see the look. The dream's better than the real thing, though. You take it from me.

# 3

HOWARD CELEBRATED MYRTLE coming to stay with us for a bit by putting on a really big sort of midnight matinée which scared the daylights out of Myrtle and made her take sleeping tablets. At about five past twelve by the luminous alarm-clock Howard woke me up by laughing very loud and nudging me hard as though we were watching something which he thought very funny at the pictures. Then he started burbling a lot of nonsense words, then he seemed to settle down again to sleep and I said 'Thank God' to myself. But I said it a lot too soon, because almost right away Howard was at it again, but this time not laughing, just the opposite, howling out loud, though it wasn't real crying. From her room next door Myrtle called in a frightened voice:

'Is he all right?' I replied, kind of soothing:

'Yes, yes, take no notice, he's often like this. You get back to sleep.'

'Oh,' she went, a bit worried. Then Howard cried out, in a very clear voice, 'If you can't clean the window, then smash it.' And then he laughed in a nasty kind of way, as it might be in a horror film. I wondered what he meant by that, because it seemed to mean something, but I found out soon enough, of course, what it meant. Then he groaned and then he bawled out more nonsense and then he started to get up. Now I knew it was no good stopping him doing that, and I knew that it was really dangerous if I tried to pull him back into bed, because that might wake him up and the shock might kill him, but what I was frightened of was Howard going next door and getting into Myrtle's bed, without meaning to of course, and that causing a lot of trouble one way or another.

So I thought the best thing to do was to follow him. Anyway, Howard, sort of humming to himself, tottered all round the room in the dark, but not banging himself too much against anything, more like a bat really, and put the light on. It was amazing how he could do that, with far less fumbling than he would have done it with when he was awake. When the light was on I could see him standing by the door in his pyjamas, kind of smiling and humming away still, with his eyes open but glazed, sort of. Then Myrtle called again:

'Are you sure everything's all right there?'

'Yes,' I called back. Then I thought. I called, 'That door of yours won't lock, but you'd better put a chair behind it or something just in case he takes it into his head to pay you a visit.' Then you could hear her dashing out of bed going 'Oh oh oh' and padding in her bare feet to do what I said.

By this time Howard was on the landing, switching all the lights on he could find, as though it was a party. Then he was going downstairs, singing away this time, a sort of long song with no words and no real tune to it, it would have got nowhere near the top ten, but that's being a bit silly, really, and cruel. Poor old Howard. I followed him downstairs, having put my dressing-gown on, and he switched on all the lights downstairs, doing it so properly that you'd have sworn he was awake. Having got all the lights on, he decided he'd go into the living-room, that is, the room where we used to sit most of the time and eat and watch the TV and so on, only using the best room on special occasions like Christmas or if anybody called. I followed him into the living-room and there he went to the sideboard, opened the cupboard part of it and took out the bottle of port we had there and put this on the dining-table, also two glasses. Then, you can believe this or believe it not, just as you please, it makes no difference to what actually happened anyway, he opened the top drawer and took out the packet of playing cards, opened it, sat down at the table, still sort of singing to himself and with the smile on his face, and dealt out, believe it or not, four hands for a game of cards. He took one of these hands himself and seemed to look at it in glazed sort of way. Then he seemed to look at the other people who he was supposed to be playing cards

19

with, then he waited. When nobody else seemed to play a card Howard threw down his cards on the table and began to cry like a little child. Then he went over to the fireside chair he used to sit on and picked up the *Daily Window* and looked as if he was reading it, though his eyes were all screwed up with crying. But you couldn't see any tears. He was holding the paper in both hands, sort of stretching it out, so that the back page was in his left hand and the front page was in his right, so you could see both the front page and the back page at the same time. On the back page you could see where it said about eighty-nine people being killed in an air crash, an air-liner having come down somewhere in America, and on the front page you could see just the picture of this film-star Rayne Waters showing a lot of bosom and holding up the baby she'd just had (her second one, and the whole world was supposed to know about it, it was so important) and the headline was MY ITSY BITSY BOOFUL. And there was Howard crying away. It seemed funny, somehow, as if he was crying away at what was on the front page and back page of the *Daily Window*, because I suppose there was really nothing to cry about there, the two pages seeming to say that even though eighty-nine people get killed, still that's put right by a little child being born, and it was right to have the child being born on the front page and the people dying on the back page. I could see nothing wrong with that. But of course Howard couldn't either, being asleep and not being able to see a thing, but crying away with a really loud boo hoo noise as he held the paper in front of him.

Then all of a sudden Howard gave a kind of sigh, put the paper down, got up sighing and walked straight out of the room, not putting anything away or turning the light off. I followed him and saw him going straight upstairs, not touching any of the lights, leaving them there to burn away all night for all he cared, but I put them off as I followed him. He went into our bedroom peaceful as a lamb and got into bed and was soon breathing away quite peaceful, leaving it to me to turn all the lights off. He made no more trouble that night, but it must have scared our Myrtle silly, what he'd done already or rather the noises he'd made. Anyway, Myrtle seemed to have taken a tablet or something, because she was breathing quite peacefully now and there was only me left awake, which in a way wasn't fair, as I had my work to go to the next day and Myrtle could lie in bed like a lady if she wanted to.

But in the morning Myrtle was up with the two of us, coming down to breakfast in a very snazzy housecoat, quilted turquoise, with her sherry-coloured hair done up in a ribbon, while Howard and I were fully dressed for going out to work. Howard, of course, didn't remember a thing about the night before and he looked quite bright-eyed and rested. We used to get up at seven to give us plenty of time. I'd always got the dinner for the oven ready the night before, and this time it was a sort of hot pot, chops and onions and sliced potatoes in layers, and I put this in the oven, with the timer fixed properly, so as not to forget it, before I did the breakfast. Howard always believed in what he called a good breakfast – egg and bacon or sausages, just the same as it might be supper, breakfast and supper calling for the same sort of thing to eat, which is funny when you come to think of it and needs thinking out. I did two slices of gammon and a fried egg for Howard and for me cornflakes was good enough. Myrtle had ideas of her own and had brought with her a bottle of PLJ and she had a glass of this and then made herself some very thin toast and she lowered herself enough to drink some of the tea I'd made for Howard and me, but without milk or sugar. When we'd sat down to breakfast the postman came and there was a letter for Howard. He frowned over the envelope a long time, letting his egg and gammon get cold, neither opening the letter nor eating his breakfast. 'Come on,' I said, 'let's know who it's from.'

'It's from the television people,' Howard said. He showed us the envelope with the name of the television company in posh lettering in the top left-hand corner. 'They've been long enough about it,' he said.

'Oh, Howard,' I said angrily, and I stamped my foot under the table, 'do open it and see what it's about.' So then he opened it and he read it very slowly, eating his breakfast with his fork in his right hand, in the Yank way of eating. Then he passed it to me without saying anything, and I read it and I saw what he meant by saying they'd been long enough about it. For Howard had been very sly, and he'd written in to be on the *Over and Over* quiz programme, oh, nearly a year before, and now at last here they were saying he was to be on it in just a fortnight's time and that they'd pay his fare to London and they wished him every success in the show. 'Well,' I said, gasping, 'that's marvellous, isn't it? Isn't that marvellous, Howard? That's wonderful, isn't it, Myrt?' But of course Myrtle didn't know what I was so excited about till I handed the letter over to her. She read the letter but she didn't get excited at all. She gave Howard a sort of sour look as if to show that he'd no right to put on the sort of frightening midnight performance he did and then come down not to a punishment but to a reward, for reward it was in a way, Howard being a good man all the time and deserving some such little break for having worked hard for his wife and his home, and he must have suffered too, somewhere deep inside him, otherwise we wouldn't have this walking and talking in the still watches of the night. I said, pretending to scold, but very very pleased really, of course:

'Why didn't you say, Howard? Why did you never breathe a word of it to your own wife? Just writing off slyly like that and not saying a thing about it.'

'Well,' said Howard, 'I didn't want you to think me a fool, which you might have done, the odds against a chance to appear on such a show being very long. And I was a bit ashamed myself, really, writing off. I'd never done such a thing before.'

Myrtle sort of sniffed and said, 'Books it says here. It says you'll be answering questions about books and their authors.'

'That's right. That's my idea.'

'Well, what do you know about books?' That was nasty, really, but Myrtle had the idea that books were all right for a man like Michael, her husband, who worked in a typewriter shop, but were all wrong for somebody who sold used cars. And it was true we didn't have many books in our house, while Myrtle and her husband belonged to some Book Club which sent you books you might or might not want to read every month or something. But Howard went to the local library sometimes, but I never knew what books he read, because I was never encouraged at school to be very interested in books. And you could see that Myrtle was jealous as anything at Howard being on the TV when she herself could have shown off her glamour and her low-cut bosom, flapping her eyelashes, but that sherry-coloured hair, of course, would not be able to be seen, TV being only black and white so far. Anyway, it was up to her, wasn't it, to write off to the TV people like Howard had done, but she didn't have the brains for a quiz show (no, that's silly to say that, when you see what people you get on those shows). No, she was lazy, that was it, too lazy to do anything, quite ready to believe that somebody might stop her in the street and say, 'My God, that face, that figure. You *must* be on TV right away,' and then shout 'Taxi, taxi.' Everything must be done for her, she do nothing herself. Howard said:

'Enough. I've read a bit. What I read I remember. Besides, I look a lot at those big books in the library, books full of facts. With any luck at all,' and he said this more gloomily than pleased, 'I shall get through to the thousand pounds.'

'Oh, Howard,' I cried, leaving my cornflakes untouched, 'won't that be marvellous?' Myrtle said:

'Perhaps you'll be able to pay some big doctor or other to cure you of carrying on in your sleep, such not being covered by the National Health.' That was a nasty thing to say. Howard looked a bit bewildered, not quite understanding. He said:

'I don't quite get that. What do you mean by that?'

'Hardly got a wink of sleep with your talking all night,' said Myrtle. 'I had to take *three* of these tablets.' Then she pulled out of her housecoat pocket a really huge bottle of brown tablets, there must have been about a hundred of them. I said:

'Now stop it, Myrtle. We don't want any of that, not first thing in the morning we don't.'

'If you don't like me talking in my sleep,' said Howard, in the very tough way he could have at times, 'you know what

23

you can do about it. It's my house, this is, and I'll do what I like in it, waking or sleeping.'

'It's not your house,' said Myrtle, stupid and bold as brass. 'You pay rent to the Council for it, same as we do for our flat. You're lucky in your neighbours, that's all I can say.' She said no more, and a good thing too. You could see that this TV letter and Howard going to answer quiz-questions about books had riled her properly. She'd gone too far, I thought, without her saying any more, so I said, not wanting a row:

'Enough, enough. Let's get these dishes in the sink, I've got to be at work at half-past eight.' I hated to come home to unwashed dishes but I wasn't going to ask Myrtle to earn her bit of keep by doing them. In a way you had to feel very sorry for Myrtle. I think Howard saw too that she had a lot to be unhappy about while we two were as happy as pigs, for he said nothing more, he just smiled in a faint sort of way and buckled to with the dishes.

Well, this was an eventful day, or anyway the front and back ends of the day were exciting. The middle chunk, which was most of the day, was just work. But when Howard and I came home for our dinner we found that Myrtle had gone out but had not left a note to say where she'd gone or when she'd be back, which was rude. In the evening when we came home we found that Myrtle had come back in the meantime (she had Howard's key) and was sitting sobbing by the fire. I asked her what was the matter and Howard was very kind and gentle too, but we couldn't get a word out of her for quite a time. So I got the tea ready and Myrtle consented to have a cup, crying into it. And then bit by bit we managed to drag the story out of her, which was that she'd gone back to their flat to get her bottle of after-bath freshener, at least that was her story, and when she got there she found a big piece of paper written on by her husband Michael, saying IF YOU THINK YOU CAN JUST COME BACK WHEN YOU FEEL LIKE IT YOU'RE MISTAKEN FOR IF I NEVER SEE YOU AGAIN THAT WILL BE TOO SOON. Well that seemed to have got her good and mad for she went straight round to the shop where Michael worked and raised all hell in the shop before the customers too, which was a silly thing to do but understandable. Anyhow, according to her it was all over now between them, but you could see that wasn't really so or she wouldn't have been in such a state. Howard and I tried to comfort her, but she wouldn't have any of that, she just wanted to be left alone with her grief, as she put it, but later on she had another cup of tea and even one quarter of a Harris's Pork Pie. We got her calmed down a lot and then we had the TV on, thinking it might distract her mind a bit, but it was unlucky that all the programmes that evening were the same sort of thing. There was the series COPPER'S NARK, and in it this week a woman tried to do herself in because her husband had gone off and left her, and that started poor old Myrt off again. Then there was a bit of a variety show which Howard said was really depressing, though I thought it was rather pretty and funny really, then we had this play and it was the same sort of thing as the COPPER'S NARK thing we'd just had, with a husband and wife quarrelling like mad and throwing the milk jug and then the husband took a knife to her and she ran away from him screaming and then she fell through the banister-rails which were broken. This time Myrtle watched very calmly and her face looked very pale and all washed-out in the light that was coming out of the TV. And then she said she'd like to go to bed and try to sleep a bit, so we said that was perhaps the best thing for her to do so we said good-night to her and I started to get supper for just Howard and me. And then Howard said:

'Funny girl, isn't she? A real suffering soul I'd call her, the sort of girl that's never been happy in her life.'

'Oh, we were both happy together,' I said, 'when we were kids. A real tomboy she was then. Happy as the day is long.' But, as I was making the toast, I couldn't help feeling that it seemed very queer Myrtle just going up quietly to bed like that and lying quietly upstairs, as if there was nobody upstairs at all. At least, that's what it felt like. But then I found I was letting the toast burn so I got on with making the supper and left Myrtle to her own devices, as they say. So Howard and I had our supper which was spaghetti romana tonight on toast, and then I went to the kitchen to bring in some chocolate biscuits of a new kind I'd brought home that day (chocolate one side and like icing sugar on the other). But

I couldn't help feeling that something might be a bit wrong with poor Myrt, so I went upstairs and found Myrtle lying in bed with the full light on, though she herself was out like a light and snoring in a very peculiar way. By the side of the bed was this bottle of brown tablets that had been nearly full that morning and now a fair number of tablets had gone out of it. It wasn't hard to put two and two together and I didn't like the look of this at all, nor the sound of this very peculiar snoring either. 'Howard, Howard,' I called downstairs, leaning over the banisters, 'come up here quick.' He could tell there was something wrong, because he came leaping up, shaking the whole house. He came into Myrtle's bedroom and sort of nodded as he saw her there, snoring away in this quiet way, lying on her back with her best nightdress on. He said:

'I see what she's done. Poor girl. She looks really peaceful now.' He put his thumb in her eye to lift up the eyelid and see what was going on underneath, and the eye looked very blank towards the head of the bed. He sort of nodded again. 'Just look at her face,' he said. 'All the worries and the anxieties ironed away. All her cantankerousness and jealousies and dissatisfactions with her mode of life. She looks sort of beautiful now, at peace if you see what I mean.'

I looked at Howard astonished. 'Aren't you going to do anything about it?' I said. 'She might be dying for all we know. Oughtn't we to force something down her throat to make her bring them all up or something? I don't like this at all.'

'We can't do anything now,' said Howard. 'She's too far gone. Whatever she's got down there in her stomach – which, of course, as you can see, is those tablets – won't come up without using a stomach pump on her.'

'Well, then,' I said, dancing up and down, 'ring up the doctor or get an ambulance, do something. She's my sister.' Without thinking I got down on the bed and started to shake poor Myrtle as though that might bring her awake, saying, 'Wake up, love. Come on, love, Janet's here.' Howard said:

'Who are we to interfere with people's decisions? She'd made up her mind to put an end to it all, and that's what she *has* done. No more trouble for her. No more worry about her husband or her looks or her clothes or the cost of fish. No more dirt and tripe and corruption from the TV and the *Daily Window*. She's well out of it all now. She's been a very brave girl and she's made the right decision.'

Howard was just standing there, swaying a bit, looking a bit as he looked in those sleep-walking acts of his, a bit glazed round the eyes. There was also something a bit like a hypnotist's look about him so that I stood there for it might have been a whole minute looking at him with my mouth open. Then I snapped out of it. I said, 'Aren't you going to do anything? Aren't you going to ring anybody up? Or are you going to leave it all to me?'

'She won't thank you for disturbing her rest,' said Howard. 'Quiet sleep and a sweet dream when the long trick's over. A right trick it is, too. More of a joke than a trick, but a trick it is, too, a dirty trick of somebody or other.' And he just stood there, sort of fascinated, looking down on poor Myrtle.

'Oh, you –' I said, and I dashed out and downstairs and got my coat and my handbag and went out, the telephone box only being at the corner of the street. I'd never done this sort of thing before, but I'd seen enough TV to know that I had to dial 999, which I did, and I asked for the ambulance service and please hurry, and I gave our address. Then I found I had no coppers to ring up our own doctor, who was Doc Kilmartin, only sixpences and other bits of silver. But coming down the street were a couple of lads in Italian suits and winkle-pickers and all the rest of it, so I put my head out of the phone-box and said, 'Can you give me change for sixpence, very urgent?' One of these lads, very pimply and blackheady, poor boy, said I was a slick chick or something, but there was no harm in either of them, poor lads, and they managed to give me four pennies in exchange for sixpence. So then I rang up Doc Kilmartin.

I got back to our house and there was Howard still standing in Myrtle's bedroom, smoking a cigarette though, and Myrtle was even deader out than before, because you couldn't hear any of that snoring. Howard was sort of drinking her in, muttering to himself, and for the first time since we'd married, for the first time since I'd known him for that matter, I felt that there was something in Howard that I didn't understand

and that I was a bit afraid of. Doc Kilmartin came round and spoke in a very severe Scottish way about what Myrtle had done and it was reprehensible or some such word, and then the ambulance arrived in all its glory, bells ringing away and lights flashing, and two men came up with a stretcher. So Myrtle was taken away to Bradcaster Royal Infirmary, lying as still as death and not knowing what was going on at all, and I went with her, leaving Howard at home. The people in the street didn't come out to see what was going on, as they would have done in the old nosy days before TV. They were too busy watching. Emergency Ward Ten would be far more real to them than any real emergency like this one.

# 4

WHEN MYRTLE WAS admitted into Bradcaster Royal
Infirmary they got the stomach-pump to her and got it all up,
but she stayed dead out. A young doctor with glasses and very
Brylcreemed glossy black hair came into the sort of lobby where
I was waiting and rang up some other part of the Infirmary to
say they were admitting a bad case of barbarous or barbituric
or something poisoning, then they asked me for details about
Myrtle and where was the bottle of tablets that she'd tried to
do herself in with. Back home, I said, which wasn't much help,
and then I remembered that Michael, her husband, had better
be got in touch with. They weren't on the phone, Michael and
Myrtle, but the police station was just round the corner from
their flat, so the station was rung up and told to send a copper
round to tell him she was in hospital, but to break the news
in a gentle sort of way. And then I asked if they were going
to get the police to take any action, remembering that this
attempted suicide was still a crime, but they said no, there was
far too much attempted suicide these days and the probation
officers would be run off their feet dealing with them, having
far more important business to deal with, especially the gangs
who didn't want to die, far from it, just the opposite in fact.

Michael wasn't very long in coming, and he came rushing in
as in some TV programme where the husband comes rushing
in to see his wife who's just been admitted to hospital, and he
looked handsome, as was the intention, but handsome in a
sort of plump softy sort of way. He kept saying, 'My wife,
my poor dear wife, oh, where is she?' like Armchair Theatre,
but was told that he couldn't see her and wouldn't be able
to till next morning, when it was hoped she would have come

29

round, but they wanted to have a little talk with him, and you could see from their stern looks that they were going to blame it all on Michael. Before they took Michael away, though, Michael turned on me and would have turned on Howard if he'd been there (and I still say he *should* have been there) to say we'd no right to let her do a thing like that, she'd never done a thing like that in her own home, and it was very funny that she should only decide to try a thing like this when staying with us, and that we must have been upsetting her, and so on. I do wish that Howard could have bashed him for saying that, there and then, but Howard wasn't there and had let me down. Anyhow, I turned back on Michael and gave him a bit, so that things got very loud and we were asked to shut up. Then I left the Infirmary with my nose in the air and got a bus and went straight home, blazing.

Not to make too long a story of it (though that's the thing Myrtle would dearly have liked, to have this her story and not mine and Howard's) Myrtle was let out of the Infirmary a few days later, right as rain, the psychiatrist having had a heart-to-heart with her, and with Michael also, and the two were all lovey-dovey once more. But it wasn't long before they were at it again, though I don't think Myrtle ever tried the suicide lark any more. For one thing, those tablets disappeared, God knew where to, and there was no gas in Myrtle's flat and she'd have been too much of a coward to try jumping out of the window or sticking the bread-knife into herself or slashing her wrists with Michael's razor-blades. (Anyway, Michael had an electric razor.) And I know for a fact that Myrtle's own doctor would not let her have any more sleeping-tablets, not even if she was rigid with insomnia, at least not as many as he'd let her have before, which had been foolish of him and I think he knew it. Although what I think had really happened was that there had been a mistake in the prescription, perhaps a nought being added where it should not have been. Or something. Anyway, I must get on with the story of Howard and me. (Or, as poor Miss Spenser at school would say, Howard and I.)

Howard spent a lot of time in the evenings with his books,

and sometimes he would sit in the Public Library with the big books they wouldn't let him take away. But at home it was amazing to see him. He'd open a book at a page full of dates and facts and then just sort of *photograph* the page. Click, and you knew he'd got it. But he found time to relax, too. In fact, he seemed very confident of his chances in the quiz show, and it was me who got more and more excited day by day. One night, on the BBC TV, they had a programme about films and there was a visit to Hollywood. We were shown round the fabulous mansion on Sunset Boulevard of Miss Rayne Waters, who I've already mentioned, a very sunburnt bosomy star, a nice girl perhaps really, but you couldn't help not liking her silly giggle when she kept saying, 'I guess so,' and 'Surely, surely,' and 'Well, I guess that's just the way things arrre, he he he.' You'd think, though, watching her take this BBC man round her fabulous mansion, that she could have afforded to buy herself a brassière, said she cattily. At the gates of her mansion there was an electronic thing for opening the gates automatically, and there was a telephone by which you could say who you were and ask if you could come in, and it was Rayne Waters herself who said, 'Surely, surely.' It didn't seem to me that the house was in very good taste, though, when we were taken round it. It was a sort of mixture of different styles of furnishing, with Chinese and Old English in the same room, and an indoor swimming-pool as well as an outdoor one, with hearts and arrows decorating everywhere, and I LOVE YOU done in diamonds on the wall of each of the twenty-four bathrooms. There was a TV set in every room, each TV set disguised as something else, such as a fireplace in one room, the whole house being of course centrally heated, and in another room the TV set was high up on the wall with a picture frame round it. (Why can't you say *square it?*) We watched this, and then Howard came out with one of his surprising remarks. He said:

'The money I'm going to get is not to be spent on anything of a permanent nature. If I won ten million pounds on one of these quiz shows it would all have to go on things that are to be, in a manner of speaking, *burnt up*. That is to say, expendable. Clothes for you, of course, because you've got to wear something proportionable to the expending that you'll be doing. The time for buying things of a permanent kind is all finished, you mark my words. Money is to be burnt up on living and not to be saved at all or converted into ornaments or furnishings or things of that nature.'

Well, I could see his point, but Howard had always been house-proud, and I should have thought he'd have wanted to buy, say, a new dining-room suite or a Hi-fi or really good curtains for the front room. But he never said now, 'When I win the money we'll have something better on the wall than those pot ducks.' He was changing inside in a queer sort of way, was Howard, but I trusted him.

And so the time came for Howard's big chance, and he was just as confident the night before as he had been all the way along. The night before he asked me to test him on Shakespeare's plays, who were the characters in them and when they were written and so on, and so I had this book and I asked him the questions out of it. He answered every one absolutely right without turning a hair. Then he came out with one of his queer outbursts. He said, 'Aaaaah, it must have been a damned sight better to live in those days than in these. I mean, they were all red-blooded men and women in those days, drinking down their ale by the gallon – and it was strong ale then, I can tell you – and jogging along on horseback instead of smoking a fag at the wheel of a car, and not reading a lot of lies and tripe put out by the *Daily Window* and gawping at the telly every evening. And no Polaris missiles and all that. Just clean honest healthy living with barrels of sack and canary, and kids looking up to their parents and not treating them like dirt and calling them squares from Cubeville. And when there was war everybody was in it fighting properly with swords and drawing blood and chopping off heads in a decent clean sort of way, not smashing people who've done no harm to anyone with hydrogen bombs and the like. And when they sang songs they were decent good songs with sensible words, not the bloody tripe you get now with a million records sold to the teenagers. All right,' he said, though I hadn't said a word, 'you can say it was unhygienic and they were deprived of the bloody blessings of wrapped bread and slices of bacon you can see through all done up in polythene, and they had no washing-machines and central heating, but it was still a better life than this one we're living now.'

'How do you know that?' I said. 'You never lived then, so how do you know?'

'I know,' he shouted. 'I just know, that's all.'

He was in one of those moods when it was no good arguing with him. We'd not done any Shakespeare at the secondary mod, because the teachers said we wouldn't like it and we'd get bored. They never gave us a chance to see whether we'd get bored or not. But I'd seen pictures of those days, with their ruffs and long hair and beards and what-not, so that the men like Sir Walter Raleigh and Sir Francis Drake looked like sort of beatniks dressed up for a fancy-dress party. And men wearing ear-rings, too. I got a sort of feeling of darkness and cruelty and very bad smells. And here was Howard crying it up, as though he was trying to sell it. Like one of his used cars.

Well, the time had come for Howard to go off to London. He had the day off, of course, perhaps his boss thinking that for Howard to be on the TV would boost his trade for him, so he made no trouble about giving him the day off. You can be sure that I'd spread the news all round the Supermarket a long time before, and the people in Shining Shoe Lane were already very sick about it, some of them. We wondered whether perhaps I ought to go up to London with Howard and appear on the programme, just standing next to him, sort of competing with the glamorous girls who fetched and carried the questions, but we decided it would be better for me to stay at home and watch. It would make it seem somehow more *real* that way.

## 5

'AND NOW,' CRIED the American or Irishman with the pointy sort of a face, 'a big hand for our next competitor.' And he led the clapping and an electric organ played a sort of march and there, led on by a brunette in a low-cut costume, fishnet stockings right up to her bottom as though she was a dancer, him very grim and her smiling enough to make her teeth drop out, there he was, my Howard in his best suit, marching on.

I'd been so nervous all that evening waiting for it to come on that I'd been really sick, that is to say I'd actually been sick after my tea, everything coming up clean as a whistle. But after a bit of a rest I felt better, so I went upstairs and made up very carefully and put on my black evening dress which was backless and came downstairs and sat with my back to the fire for a bit. Then, a good hour before *Over and Over* (it was called that, by the way, because you were supposed to go on making money over and over again, or something like that) I had the TV switched on. My heart was a bit in my mouth. Supposing something went wrong, like the tube suddenly going just as the show started. Supposing there was an electricity cut. Supposing the electricity fused, and I was hopeless at putting things like that right, that being Howard's job. I felt a bit cross because Howard wasn't there, but then I saw that was silly. Anyway, as you can tell, everything went all right. I was most proud of all when they showed the News, with Harold Macmillan and President Kennedy and so on, and the Shah of Persia and Adam Faith, knowing that now Howard had sort of joined their number, being on TV.

Well, Howard was second on, the first competitor being a

chinny old woman who was very proud of being eighty-nine or some such age and insisted on doing a dance and showing her bloomers. Of course, the quiz-master went along with her and asked her easy questions about cookery, and helped her to get the right answers, then he put his arms round her and kissed her and everybody cheered. So it was going to be a bit difficult for Howard, Howard being a serious type and not likely to want to dance or grin like an ape or make silly jokes. Anyway, I remember every word that was spoken that night. First the quiz-master said, 'What's your name, sir?' and Howard told him, then the quiz-master said, 'A little louder, please,' so Howard firmly boomed it out so that the ornaments on the mantelpiece shook. 'And are you married, sir?' Howard said he was. 'And your job, sir?' Howard said he sold used cars and for some reason that got a very big round of applause. To this day I wonder why. 'And what are your hobbies?' asked the quiz-master. Howard said, very seriously, 'I've only one hobby, and that is my wife.' And that brought the house down practically. The quiz-master was clapping away and leading the cheering, and I felt silly but proud. I hoped very much Myrtle was watching. I knew, of course, that she was bound to be watching, just as Mum and Pop would be, and all the neighbourhood for that matter, but Myrtle would probably say she forgot to see it, or she and Michael had a prior engagement or something. What I wanted was for Myrtle to *admit* she'd been watching and not to pretend otherwise. And I wanted her to hear that about me being Howard's only hobby. Then the quiz-master said, 'And what do you want to be asked questions about, Howard?' He'd dropped the 'sir' now and was being all matey. Howard said, 'Books.' The quiz-master called the girl with the fishnet stockings and the big smile as though the show was her show, and he asked her to bring the questions about Books. So then it started and my heart thumped so I could almost *taste* it.

'First question for one pound,' said the quiz-master. I suppose it would sound more matey, seeing that *he* decided to be all matey, to call him by his name, which was Laddie O'Neill, really a dog's name. Anyway, Laddie said, 'Which would be better for breakfast, Shakespeare or Bacon?'

'That's a bloody silly question.'

The audience didn't know what to make of that, and I blushed because that was typical of Howard, but the quizmaster, that is to say Laddie, just laughed it off and said, 'It's meant to be a silly question, because the first question always is.' Then Howard turned on a big smile and said:

'All right, Bacon, but I'd like something Shelley with it.' Nobody in the audience saw that, but Laddie yelled his head off and said, 'Very good, very good indeed, meaning, of course, that an egg is shelly. Excellent. And now, for two pounds, question number two. What three sisters wrote books under the name of Bell?' Howard said:

'The Brontë sisters. That is to say, Charlotte Brontë, 1816 to 1855, Emily Brontë, 1818 to 1848, and Anne Brontë, 1820 to 1849. They called themselves, respectively that is, Currer Bell and Ellis Bell and Acton Bell.'

Everybody was a bit stunned by this, you could tell that, and poor old Laddie O'Neill's jaw just dropped as if he'd suddenly died standing up. 'Oh,' he said, 'right. But I haven't got all that written down here.'

'All that's correct,' said Howard. 'You can take it from me.' And he looked very burly and sure of himself.

'Question number three,' said Laddie, 'for four pounds.' And he began to read the question like a little child, stumbling a bit over the words. You could see he didn't know much about it. But he was a nice helpful sort of a man, and you couldn't help liking him. I only wished Howard would be a bit more nice and not be so serious and stern. Then, while he was waiting for the question, Howard suddenly winked at me, and, like a fool, I winked back. 'For four pounds,' said Laddie. 'This is in three parts and you've got to get them all right. Name the authors of the following three seventeenth-century books. *Hesperides. Religio Medici. Tetrachordon.*' I can't show you how he pronounced these names, but he stuttered at them and stumbled over them and tried to make a bit of a joke of them with the audience. But Howard put him right on the way to pronounce them, and said: '*Hesperides* was the secular poems of Robert Herrick, 1591 to 1674. *Religio Medici* or *A Doctor's Religion* was by Sir Thomas Browne,

1605 to 1682. *Tetrachordon* was a book on divorce written by John Milton.' He smiled in a thin-lipped way, then he said, 'Sorry. 1608 to 1674.'

Now, you could see the audience wasn't too sure how to take all this, Howard knowing so much and coming out with it too pat. What an audience likes is for you to get something wrong and have to be helped, or to be a bit slow in answering, but there Howard was, full of it all and giving information he wasn't called on to give, so that it looked as if he was showing off. I wanted to shout to him about that, but of course there was nothing I could do but tear my handkerchief to bits in my teeth and groan a bit. Then Laddie O'Neill said, 'You honestly needn't tell us all these dates, you know, Howard.' He put his arm round Howard. You could see he was really a very nice man. 'We admire your knowledge and so on, Howard, but just give us the answer and no more. Okay?' Howard smiled at that and then the audience decided to be very nice to Howard and they clapped and cheered. An audience is a very funny thing, really. 'Right,' said Laddie. 'For eight pounds.' And he cleared his throat. 'You're to give me the names of the authors of the following lines of poetry. Ready?' And he read them out in a very stiff sort of voice.

'Music has charms to soothe a savage breast.'

'That's William Congreve,' said Howard. 'From his play *The Mourning Bride*.'

'An honest man's the noblest work of God.'

'Alexander Pope,' said Howard. 'His *Essay on Man*.'

This was getting monotonous. 'The paths of glory lead but to the grave,' said Laddie.

'Thomas Gray. *Elegy in a Country Churchyard*.' And then Laddie O'Neill gave Howard a bit of shock. He said:

'I fried an egg upon the sidewalk hot.'

Howard's face dropped a mile. 'Pardon?' he said. And my heart dropped, too. Howard didn't know it. Laddie repeated the line. Howard nearly cried. He didn't know, he didn't know. He said:

'I don't know.'

'Quite right,' said Laddie. 'How can you be expected to know when I've only just made it up?' And then everybody collapsed with mirth and relief and whatnot. For there were only three parts to the question and Howard had got them all right, but Laddie was just having a bit of a game with him. And it wasn't a bad idea, really, because Howard wasn't so cocky now as he had been. My poor clever Howard. But it wasn't cleverness, as he always said. It was his poor photographic brain.

'Right,' said Laddie. 'The next one's for sixteen pounds. Here it is. And a mouthful it is, too. What were the two big eighteenth-century literary hoaxes, and who were the people responsible for them?'

'Chatterton was responsible for the Rowley poems,' said Howard, in a humble sort of way now, 'and Macpherson was the real author of Ossian.'

'Correct,' yelled Laddie, and the audience cheered. Everybody was on very good terms now. 'And for thirty-two pounds,' said Laddie, and you could see he had his eye on the clock, 'give me the names of the dead people in whose memory the following poems were written.' Then he rattled off the names. '*In Memoriam. Lycidas. Adonais. Thyrsis.*' And Howard rattled off his answers just as fast:

'Hallam. Edward King. Keats. A.H. Clough.'

And the house was brought down again and things were thrown in the air and Howard was given his thirty-two pounds in notes by the fishnet girl who put her arm round him. 'Back in a few minutes,' yelled Laddie O'Neill, and then the commercials came on. The way they did this programme was to do a few more people in the second half and then bring back whoever had won thirty-two pounds, and they could keep that, nothing could take that away from them, and if this person wanted to qualify for what they called The Big Money then he or she had to answer one hard question. If they got the right answer to this, then the person, he or she, they, would come back the next week and try and get up to five hundred pounds. Then the week after that would be for one thousand pounds, and that's what Howard looked like getting if everything went all right. I was suddenly very hungry as soon as they brought on the commercials, what with advertising tinned Steak and Kidney Pudding and then tinned

38

Risotto and whatnot. So I made myself a very quick sandwich of a wedge of corned beef left over from the morning when I'd made Howard sandwiches to take with him on the train, two big chunks of bread and this corned beef in between, with mustard on. I must have looked a bit queer, sitting there in my glamour, all alone in the house, with this whacking great big sandwich, but there was nobody to see me except the people in the commercials. Then the second part of *Over and Over* came on and there were two or three very dull people who all went off with either four pounds or eight, I wasn't very interested, and then it was Howard once more. When he came on he got a big loud burst of applause and I felt very proud. They made him climb on to a sort of pedestal with spotlights on it and a fishnet-stocking girl on either side to help him down, I supposed, both of them showing every tooth they'd got, and a lot more besides. Then they made a very big thing of bringing the envelope with the special question in it, the idea being, as I said, that if he got this right then he could go on next week to sixty-four, then a hundred and twenty-five, then two hundred and fifty, then five hundred pounds. So my heart was in my mouth, all mixed up with corned-beef sandwich, as they played sort of eerie music on the electric organ and Laddie O'Neill opened the envelope up, Laddie looking to me now like a real old friend. Laddie said:

'Here is the question which, if you get it right, qualifies you for The Big Money next week. Are you ready?' Yes, we were all ready. Howard was up there in the spotlights like a statue wearing a best suit, still as anything, but you could see he was a bit nervous. That was because they made such a solemn sort of occasion of it all. 'Right,' said Laddie. 'Here it is. Listen carefully.' And he read the question in a very solemn way, as if this was all happening in church. He said, 'You are asked to give two examples of tet – tet – tet –'

'Tetralogies?' said Howard.

'Tetralogies. Thank you. My false teeth aren't fitting very well tonight,' Laddie said, winking at the audience. Then, very serious again, he said: 'Two examples of tetralogies from the work of modern novelists. Thirty seconds to answer, starting now.' So Howard said, right away and very clear:

'Well, there's the Alexandria Quartet, as it's called, by Lawrence Durrell, and there's the Tietjens tetralogy by Ford Madox Ford.'

And of course he was right. But naturally he had to muck it all up by showing off and saying, 'In modern poetry, of course, there's T. S. Eliot with his *Four Quartets*, but you did say the novel, didn't you?' But he said this while the clapping was going on. What the silly fool didn't realise was that they'd make it really hard for him from now on. From now on he'd get the toughest questions all the professors at universities and so on could drag out of their beards. He'd really done for himself, had Howard, what with his contempt for everybody showing itself like that in his showing off. But the programme ended with Howard being helped down off his pedestal by these two glamorous grinning girls with their fishnet stockings up to their bottoms, and people cheering and Laddie clapping away with his mouth open and the electric organ playing something sort of very triumphant, almost like the second wedding march. And I was very proud.

# 6

HOWARD CAUGHT THE nine-five from Euston and so was back in the house in the very small hours of the morning when I had already been in bed for a long time and was too sleepy to say much except that I was very proud and not to show off quite so much in future. He got very hurt about that and wanted to start a long argument, but I told him to come to bed, which he did, but not before he had made me look at the thirty-two pounds he'd won. I told him they didn't look any different from other pound-notes I'd seen and to come to bed and we'd talk about it in the morning. So he came to bed and that warmed me up a lot. If there was no other reason for getting married that would be as good a reason as any, the way it keeps you warm in bed. In the morning we were both a bit tired, but we got up as usual and had our breakfast and Howard told me all about it – what it was like at the TV studios and the cameras with little red eyes on them wandering all over the place, and how everybody had been very nice. And I said, 'You watch your step, my lad, being cocky and know-all like you were.' And he had to agree about the showing-off, but he said it was more nervousness than anything else. So we went off to work, and of course everybody at the Supermarket had a bit of a say about last night, the catty ones agreeing with me (though I kept that to myself with *them*) about Howard showing off.

Howard insisted on us going out that evening in one of the cars from the Used Car Mart, dressed up a bit, to spend some of the thirty-two pounds as a celebration. Which we did, and we drank a bit too much when we'd had our dinner at the Green Man out near Willbridge, and this led, one way and another, to Howard losing his job at the Used Car Mart. Howard was a good driver, having been for a time on his national service a staff-car driver for a colonel or somebody, but he could show off a bit too much, as in the quiz programme, and he could be careless. What happened was that he drove this Bentley we were in straight into a wall just as we were coming into Pelham, although I will say the fault was not altogether his. There was another car, driven by some *real* drunk, coming whizzing out of Pelham zigzagging all over the road, and Howard swerved to avoid it and over-corrected or something, and then the car went right into this wall, though he got the brakes on almost in time or something. The two head-lamps were smashed and a big dent made in the bonnet, and this Bentley, though it was a second-hand car like all the cars at the Mart, was a bit newer than most and was supposed to be everybody's pride and joy, especially old Watts', Howard's boss. Well, as you can well imagine, next day there was a bit of a row at the Used Car Mart, especially as, to make matters worse, with the drink and all, we forgot to set the alarm and so both woke up a bit late, me with a rotten headache too. When Howard came home at dinner-time he'd walked, not driven in one of the used cars with the advertisement on, as had been his custom, and he told me he was leaving at the end of the week and to hell with bloody old Watts.

'What happened?' I asked.

'Oh,' said Howard, 'when I got in I said I was sorry about everything and that they could charge the repair job to me and so forth, but old Watts got very nasty. Jealousy, I think, more than anything else because of me being on the TV. Anyway, he said he wasn't at all satisfied, if I wanted to know, with the way things had been going, making out that he'd lost a lot of sales because of me being too honest with the customers, telling them to watch this and to watch that and if they weren't pleased with their buy to bring it back and so on, and before we knew where we were we were having a real blazing row, and what with my head being a bit rough and a nasty taste in my mouth I fairly let him have it. I told Watts what to do with his bloody nasty business and his cheating and dishonesty, and he said that I'd got too big for my boots and what call did a working-man like me have with books and answering learned questions on the telly. So I told him he was an ignorant old sod who thought only of making dishonest money and perhaps going after little girls in dark alleyways, which is true, you know, and he said he'd have me for slander and libel and whatnot. Then we sort of calmed down for a bit, though he knew I'd spoken a bit of truth and at the same time I couldn't help feeling a bit sorry for the ugly old sod, so it was agreed I work till the end of the week and then get my cards and that's that as far as the Used Car Mart's concerned, as far as I'm concerned, anyway.'

'Well, what are you going to do?' I asked.

'There's no particular hurry,' said Howard, in his very calm manner. 'There's the quiz next week and the week after that to get ready for. I could do with the time really. Some of those questions I got asked were very tough.'

'You may not get through the first stage of The Big Money,' I said. 'Next week you may be just out of it, with only thirty-two pound to show for it. Less than that now,' I said, 'after last night.'

'I've got a feeling,' said Howard, putting on his very prophetical way of speaking, 'that we won't have to worry any more. That I'm going to win this lot and more besides. If you want to you can give up your job in the Supermarket right away. There's not going to be any need for either of us to work.'

'Are you crazy?' I said. 'Even if you win the thousand quid that's not going to last for ever, is it? Besides,' I said, 'I'm not so sure that I want to give up my job. I like it there, meeting people and having a bit of gossip, and I'd have to go there anyway, wouldn't I, to do the shopping. It's a bit of life for me, a bit of the outside world,' I said.

'So,' said Howard, 'you wouldn't be happy just with me, just the two of us together?' He looked very much like a dog when he said that, sort of begging for affection. And I said:

'Oh, of course. But we mustn't lose touch, must we? I mean, the world's got to go round, hasn't it?' It seemed very funny, all that. Howard seemed to have all these interests, but that

43

was just really his photographic brain. Really, he only liked being with me, having spoken the truth on the TV when he said I was his only hobby. He never went to football or to boxing or to the new bowling-alley, like other men, or even to a pub on his own. He always wanted to be with me. Now, that was very flattering and I was pleased, as any woman ought to be, but I'd never really known anybody like Howard before and it was just a bit frightening. He'd look at me with love in his eyes sometimes, and it was just like a sort of big smouldering fire. But then, with this very bad rainy weather, I thought how nice it would be if we could be together all the time, with the door locked and good fires going in both downstairs rooms, like Christmas, and all the people at work in the outside world while we listened to Music While You Work and then Mrs Dale's Diary with the sleet lashing away at the windows and everything warm and cosy within. But there was the other side of life to think of, like meeting people and having a chat and looking at the shop-windows and the odd laugh at work with the bustle of all the shoppers with their wire baskets round you. There's always two sides to life, and I ask everybody to remember that.

The following week was very peculiar, with me going off to work and Howard staying at home. I won't deny that it made things a lot easier for me, because it did. Howard could cook in a sort of rough man's sort of way, but the plates were always hot and nothing was under-cooked – just the opposite, really, the sausages almost black – and he was a very clean washer-up. He was also very thorough with the vac and very hot on spiders' webs and dust generally. But it made me almost want to cry when he came to the door to welcome me back as soon as he heard me putting my key in the lock, Howard with one of my frilly aprons on and the kitchen full of smoke if he'd been frying something, which he normally did. And Howard always very welcoming and loving when I got home. And then Thursday came and it was time for Howard to go off to London to start The Big Money part of the quiz, still very confident and prepared to show everybody that he was a bit above selling used cars really.

Well, there I was in the evening, sitting in front of the TV with my black evening frock on. I'd made some fairly dainty sandwiches in advance and there was a bottle of British sherry, these things waiting till I should feel less nervous and not want to throw everything up. Also, I'd locked the front door and was going to pretend that there was nobody in if anybody knocked. (Some neighbour might come and say, 'Our telly's gone bust, dear, and we didn't want to miss your hubby, did we now? So we came to watch him with you.' The idea really being that they hoped he made a mess of it and it would be nice for them to have a bit of a gloat at me being so disappointed, as would only be natural.)

Anyway, my heart nearly came up and fell on the hearthrug when the words *Over and Over* came on to the screen. There was interference also from some car or other, so that the screen got full of snow and there was a loud frying noise, so that I cursed just like Howard himself would have done. But everything was all right in a bit, and the people they had on in the first half of the show were the usual stupid crowd except for one bank clerk who knew quite a lot about modern jazz and could have got on to The Big Money. But the rule was that nobody could be on it while somebody else was on it, the somebody else being Howard in this case. Then we had the commercials and I ate a couple of sandwiches and washed them down with British sherry, and when I saw Howard walking on the screen in the second half of the show I felt quite calm really. Howard looked very confident and acknowledged the loud applause with a sort of dignified bow. Then they put him in a big box with a glass door and he put head-phones on, and there was the big clock ready to tick away. And then Laddie O'Neill, who was really now like a very old friend, asked for the Big Money questions and the brunette, this week wearing flesh-coloured tights, brought them in grinning all over her face. Laddie said, very solemnly:

'And now here is the sixty-four pound question.' He cleared his throat and you could almost hear people breathing very quickly and nervously, but you couldn't hear any other sound as he said: 'I want you to give the names of four books which have the word "Golden" in the title, and also the names of the authors. Have you got that?' Howard said yes. 'Right,' said Laddie. 'Thirty seconds, starting – *now*.' And Howard said:

'*The Golden Ass*, by Lucius Apuleius. *The Golden Bough*, by Sir James Frazer. *The Golden Bowl*, by Henry James. And. And. And.' It was awful, Howard trying to think desperately, with the clock ticking away. 'And,' said Howard, '*The Golden Legend*, by Longfellow.'

Of course, everybody went mad clapping, and there was Howard saying, 'Or *The Golden Age* by Kenneth Grahame. Or *The Golden Arrow* by Mary Webb. Or *The Golden Cheronese* by –' But they shut him up then and Laddie asked him if he wanted to go on to the hundred and twenty-five pound question. Which Howard did. This time he was told he must *wait* thirty seconds before giving his answer. Laddie O'Neill said:

'The following are the *real* names of certain authors. I want you to give, for a hundred and twenty-five pounds, their pseudonyms or pen-names. Right?' Right. Then he reeled off these names and, honestly, they meant nothing to me. there were five of them, and Laddie said the whole list twice, and Howard had to hold these names in his head while he waited thirty seconds. This thirty seconds seemed like an age, and it didn't make it any better, the electric organ playing sort of spooky music while Howard was supposed to be thinking of his answers. But then he came out with them, cheerful and confident as anything:

'Armandine Aurore Lucile Dupin was known as George Sand. Mary Ann Cross was George Eliot. Charles Lamb called himself Elia. Eric Blair wrote as George Orwell. And I've forgotten the fifth. Oh dear, oh dear.' This was a terrible moment, for he wasn't allowed to be given the name again, which seemed very unfair. But just as I was going to be sick on the carpet he remembered and said, 'Oh, yes,' and I got the impression that he'd only been pretending to have forgotten, 'Samuel Clemens called himself Mark Twain.'

Well, after all the applause, he was on to the two hundred and fifty pound question, and it was not any use me feeling like a wet rag yet, because there was the five hundred pound question to come, and that would be enough for this week.

Anyway, here was the next question, and it might as well have been in Greek for all it meant to somebody like me:

'This question is in three parts. In what novels do the following characters appear? First, Glossin.'

'Scott's *Guy Mannering*,' said Howard.

'Imlac.'

'Dr Johnson's *Rasselas*,' said Howard.

'Densil Ravenshoe.' And you could see from the way he said it that that was a tough one. But Howard said:

'Easy. A novel with that name, I mean *Ravenshoe*, by Henry Kingsley.'

Honestly, and as you can see, Howard was really terrific. And only me and a few more knew, certainly nobody in that television studio knew, that it was all because of poor Howard's photographic brain. Well, when the applause had died down and Howard was asked if he'd do the five hundred pound question and said yes, you got a sort of impression that they were sharpening their axes. And then these two girls walked on not showing their legs, but wearing skirts, as though this was too solemn a business for legs to be shown. They didn't have anything to do except just stand on either side of the box where Howard was sort of imprisoned, like a decoration, and they didn't grin this time but were very serious. And then Laddie O'Neill got the five hundred pound question in his hands and he coughed and you could tell it was going to be a real stinker. But in for a penny in for a pound, and I'd rather Howard lost now than he should have been weak and taken away just the two hundred and fifty. And if he got this one I wanted him to go straight on to the end. And here it was. 'What poem,' said Laddie, 'by what royal author is written about at length by Sir W. A. Craigie in *Essays and Studies by Members of the English Association*, Volume 24?'

'A catch question,' said Howard, 'really. The only important poem written by somebody royal is *The King's Quair* by James I of Scotland, written in 1423 and 1424 while he was a prisoner in England and about the time of his marriage to –' But you couldn't hear any more from Howard, because Laddie O'Neill was dancing up and down saying it was right, it was right, and the audience was yelling away and then the programme was over and I had another week of agony in front of me before the thousand pound question, knowing full well that Howard wouldn't take the five hundred and that he'd go on to the end, and I admired him for that and loved him but also felt a bit frightened, I didn't quite know why.

# 7

As you might expect, Howard was now quite famous in Bradcaster, and people would point him out in the street. But it didn't seem to me that they pointed him out in a *nice* way, as if he was a pop-singer, but in a sort of mixed way, part admiring and part sneering, if you see what I mean, as though it was all wrong for a grown man to waste his time on book-learning, even if it did perhaps mean him winning a thousand pounds, as if it was not manly, somehow. People are very queer, really. If a man's a professor, for instance, they always think he's going to be ugly and untidy and bald and absent-minded, and I don't see any reason why that should be true. One evening in the week we went out to the French Horn, which is a pub just near the Town Centre, for a couple of drinks, and some lads in the pub recognised Howard and started to make remarks. They were more silly than offensive, really, these lads being very young in their leather jackets and tight trousers, earning good money too, as you could see from their drinks, which were Babycham and Pony and things like that, which I'd always thought to be a woman's drink, really. Anyway, they went 'Haw haw haw' to each other and 'The next question is for hondred and forty ponds,' speaking like with a potato in their mouths. But Howard just grinned at that, for they were only silly boys.

It was a pity in a way that Howard had lost his job at the Used Car Mart, because a lot of people started saying that he'd given it up because he thought he was too good for it now, and pride came before a fall, and you could see there were some who were just dying for Howard to fail on the thousand pound question. I knew all about this, because, after all, I worked at the Hastings Road Supermarket and heard people talking by the wrapped loaves shelf and near the washing powders and so on, and a lot of them didn't know who I was. And some were bold as brass and spoke right out to my face that Howard had made a grave mistake giving up his job and that it was counting his chickens and a bird in the hand was worth two in the bush, and things of that sort. I tried to keep my temper, of course, but it was a bit difficult, especially when some of the other girls at the Supermarket had their own bit of a sneer about me still working while Howard was at home poking the fire, and one girl, Edna Simons, called me 'Your ladyship'. That was uncalled for, that sort of sarcastic thing, and I turned on her nastily and would have scratched her face if she'd been worth wasting energy on, so I contented myself with upsetting the pile of tins of cut-price peaches in syrup she'd just put on the floor, and then she started to cry out like a really common thing. The whole Supermarket seemed to turn sour on me that day, and when I got home at dinner-time and saw that Howard had the place nice and clean, with the fire blazing away, and had done a sort of mixed grill of sausages, eggs, bacon, and some potatoes left over from yesterday fried up, and everything nice and hot though a bit overdone, I really felt like following what Howard had said and saying to hell with the Supermarket and then locking the front door and there'd just be the two of us by the fire all afternoon, and let the rest of the world go by, as the song said. But I went back to work in the afternoon, as usual.

When I got home in the evening Howard was sort of dancing about all over the place and shouting that he'd won, he'd won. I thought at first he'd gone crackers, because the quiz wasn't till the next day (Thursday), but then he explained. Howard, as I've already said, was always full of surprises, and what he'd done, without telling me, was to open up an account with the Turf Commission Agent, George Welbeck ('Welbeck Never Welshes'), on Station Road. He'd done that slyly in the morning and then he'd put five pounds each way on a horse called Caper Spurge, because he'd remembered once looking up Caper Spurge in the dictionary, and it had given Myrtle Spurge as having the same meaning, and Howard had thought of my sister Myrtle and put five pounds each way on this horse running in the three o'clock at Doncaster. The horse had come in, as you might expect, at a hundred to eight, so Howard certainly had some cause for rejoicing, me too, for that matter. That was typical of Howard, somehow, and yet you couldn't think of Howard as lucky. And, while I was glad about this win of his, I couldn't help feeling a bit hollow in the pit of my stomach. I don't know why, but I did. Still, perhaps this was a good omen for the following evening. Howard said it was, and he was as confident as anything.

The next morning, when the *Daily Window* came, there was a bit about Howard in it. The *Daily Window* had what it called a Telly Korner, with bits of gossip about stars appearing on TV and saying a bit about the programmes you could see that night. It said, 'In *Over and Over* tonight sacked used car salesman Howard Shirley tackles the thousand pound question on Books.' (I could see that Howard must have been talking to somebody at the television studios about being sacked, which was a silly thing to do.) It didn't say any more than that, as though the really important thing was that Howard was sacked, and it sort of upset me and made me feel that I didn't want to go to work that day. I said this to Howard and he said:

'Don't go to work. Come with me to London. When I've won and the show's over we can go out for dinner somewhere and we can stay the night in a hotel.' Well, that seemed reasonable to me, and I thought, well, I might not feel so sick being in the studio with the studio audience, instead of here watching on my own. So I said yes. Howard went to the telephone kiosk on the corner and rang up the Supermarket and left a message that I wouldn't be coming that day. At least, that's what he said he said when he came back from phoning. Actually, what he'd really said was that I wasn't going back any more to the Supermarket, but he didn't tell me that till afterwards. It was his usual sly way.

Anyway, you could see that from now on was our new life, whatever happened. We were bound to be different now, whatever happened, from what we'd been before, and it felt very strange and somehow very sad. I cooked breakfast, a good sustaining one because we'd be travelling, eggs and bacon for both of us, and after breakfast I dressed myself up very carefully in my cinnamon outfit, putting on clean underclothes underneath and not just clean either, but new, ones I hadn't worn before. And Howard put on everything clean, with very clean brown shoes, and his best suit. It felt as if we were going off to get married in a register office. I had my dyed opossum coat, and I'd made up very carefully, and I suppose we must have looked a very handsome couple as we walked to the bus. And as we walked to the bus, Howard suddenly said, 'To hell! What are we doing this for? I'll ring up for a taxi.' The bus-stop was just a bit beyond the telephone kiosk, and it was perhaps seeing the telephone kiosk that put the idea into Howard's head. Anyway, he sent me back home to wait, and then he came back, and then one of Greenfield's men arrived to take us to the station.

Howard was certainly in a very reckless mood today, or else over-confident, because when we walked into the booking hall at London Road Station he said again, 'To hell!' and then he booked first-class for us. I'd never travelled first-class before, at least not having paid for it; like everybody else I'd got into a first-class compartment with a second-class ticket, but only for very short journeys when the ticket-collector doesn't come down the train, but I'd not even done that very often. Today the train was a bit full, with a lot of business-men going up to London, and the compartment we got into had four very old and prosperous-looking men in it, reading *The Times*, but not too busy reading it to give me the old once-over. There was a sort of smell of the pantomime on Boxing Day in the compartment, porty and cigarry, and the men had mottles and blue veins all over their noses, and the veins were sticking out a mile on their hands that held their newspapers. They were old rich men going to London to see how things were on the Stock Exchange or something, or to go to a take-over bid or something like that. Howard had bought me a very snazzy magazine, *Vogue*, realising that the fivepenny kind of woman's magazines wouldn't do at all here, and he'd bought a *Times* for himself. So that was five *Timeses* in one compartment, no question of anybody saying, 'When you've finished with *Blighty* hand it over and you can have a read of my *Tit-bits*.' Howard was reading *The Times* properly, too, frowning over it, and then I had to remind myself that, after all, Howard *had* been to the grammar school and, even though his brain *was* photographic, he did know a few things and was interested in things that he never talked about with me. He was frowning over an article about Stravinsky or some such name while the train went whizzing out of the dirty town into the clean countryside and on to London.

We had a very nice lunch in the first-class dining-car, in spite of the very strong smell of sprouts that was in it. We had gravy soup, then veal cutlets with creamed potatoes and frozen peas, then cabinet pudding. We also had a half-bottle of what was called *Médoc*, and when the coffee came we had some brandy, too. I was a bit sleepy afterwards, back in the compartment, and everybody had a bit of a zizz, as they call it, while the poor engine-driver had to keep awake to drive us on to London. One of the old take-over-bid men in the compartment snored really loud. I dozed off in spite of that, and when I woke up it was dark and Howard said we were just coming into Euston. It was a bit of a surprise to me when Howard also told me that we hadn't reached our journey's end yet. We'd got to go to Charing Cross and then take a train to some suburb or other outside London, because that was where this television centre was.

When we got there eventually the television centre was a really big place, very modern, with a lot of cars and vans parked outside. The man at the big glass doors seemed to know Howard and he gave me a nice smile for myself. Then Howard, knowing his way as though he worked there, led me down corridors and at last we came to a sort of drawing-room, very deep carpets and ashtrays like big wheels of glass, and then they brought us some tea. It was very restful and everybody was very nice. Soon it was time for Howard to be taken off to be made up, and then I began to feel the old palpitations. But everybody was very nice. Very well-dressed, too.

# 8

AND WHEN AT last I met Laddie O'Neill I found him
very nice too, and really charming, and he'd been chewing
things to make his breath sweet. He had a very nice manner.
And all the time the fatal hour was drawing nearer and nearer
and I was taken to what they called the auditorium and given
a seat on the front row. People were coming in, all eager to see
this show, and I couldn't for the life of me see why anybody
should want to travel a long way, as some of these people
had done, just for this half-hour show, when they had no
personal interest in it. I mean, it was all right to look at in
your own home, so long as you had no personal interest in
it, but to come all this way was another thing. And, really,
it wasn't a very *interesting* show when you came to think of
it. Meanwhile all the people were coming in and the hands
of the clock crept on. There were monitor screens up on
the ceiling, and we could see lights flashing all over them,
and the men on the cameras were riding round and going
up in the air and then down again. I could see then that
there *was* something exciting in all that, far more exciting
than the show, except, of course, for my personal etc, etc.

Then Laddie O'Neill came to warm us up, telling a few
jokes and asking us to clap in the right places, and then
we waited and we could see on the monitor screens the
commercials before the show, then came silence, then the
letters B.A.A.D., played like music, those letters standing for
British And Affiliated Distribution, whatever that means, then
the title of the show, then we were all clapping while this
chap played the electronic organ, and the show had begun.
The woman sitting to my right kept breathing in a wheezy

sort of way, and she smelt of very strong peppermints. On my left was a little girl of about nine or ten, who didn't seem to belong to anybody. The first part of the show was the usual thing, rather silly people being clapped for knowing that twice two was four and having to be helped even with that, and one old man having to be cheered because he was eighty-eight and knew nothing about anything. And then we had to have an old charwoman full of Cockney humour, as they call it, though it just seemed like downright rudeness to me. She took her teeth out for a laugh and did a Knees Up Mother Brown with poor old Laddie O'Neill who had to pretend he was enjoying it as he'd never enjoyed anything in his life before. And then it was time for the break for the commercials. Everybody in the studio audience seemed to have got word that I was Howard's wife, and people smiled at me in a kind way as though they felt sorry for me. One old woman behind prodded me in the back and said, 'You ought to be up there with him, there's been plenty of married couples up there plenty of times.' But some man next to her, perhaps her husband, said, 'Don't talk soft, there's only room for one in them glass boxes, and she'd look a right charlie up there just standing doing nothing anyway.'

I really wanted to be sick when the curtains opened once more, and there was a kind of back-curtain with £1,000 written right across. The two girls, hostesses they were really called, came in with Howard, and there were loud claps and cheers, but I could do nothing except swallow the big lump that kept coming up, a new lump coming up for every one that I swallowed. Now these two girls had already been introduced to me before the show started and, really, they were both very nice and quite well-educated and what they did, smiling and wearing fishnet stockings, was only an act really, something they did for the money, because they said the acting profession was overcrowded and they found it very difficult to get good parts in plays. They were called Vicki and Maureen. Howard looked handsome as usual and very confident, and he bowed slightly with a little grin to acknowledge the applause. Then he was put in the glass box with a light on inside, and there was a big clock on the wall. He had to put on his headphones and Laddie O'Neill had his microphone ready and Laddie said, 'Can you hear me all right, Howard?' Howard said he could. Then Vicki brought the thousand-pound questions in an envelope. It was a very tense moment as Laddie broke the envelope open, and as he just glanced over the paper he took out you could see from his face that he knew the questions were very difficult. Then came the usual rigmarole about the time to be given for answering questions, and the first answer was to be taken as the answer Howard meant, no second shots, and think very carefully before answering. So Laddie read out the three questions in one bunch and asked Howard if he understood the questions, which Howard said he did. But to me, of course, and to everybody else in the audience the questions just meant nothing. So then Laddie began to ask each question separately and the clock started ticking away and Howard answered the questions carefully and very clearly. You might feel like asking now how it is that I know these questions and the answers to them as well, do I just remember them or something, but the fact is that there was a copy of all the questions given to Howard as a sort of souvenir, and I've kept this copy. Poor, poor Howard. Question No. 1 was this:

'Mediaeval literature. Who were the authors of the following? *Confessio Amantis; The Testament of Cresseid; The Vision of Piers Plowman.*' And Howard answered:

'John Gower; Robert Henryson; William Langland.'

That was right, of course, and there was very big applause, but it just struck me for an instant, and it was almost as if it was Howard himself thinking and not me, that it was cheap and dirty to applaud something that nobody had any idea of, that nobody cared a bit about these three men, whoever they were, and that the three men, who I all saw with beards and very old-fashioned clothes and dirty with not having bathed, were all dead and dignified and quiet and sort of despising everybody here in this studio. And I'd never read them or even heard of them and I felt sorry and mean somehow, and I got a picture in my mind of Mr Slessor our English master, so-called, with his crazy, man and his way out, and I felt sick and angry. And all this was in about one second. Question No. 2 was this:

'Elizabethan drama. Who wrote *The Shoemaker's Holiday, Bartholomew Fair* and *A New Way to Pay Old Debts*?' And Howard said:

'Thomas Dekker; Ben Jonson; Philip Massinger.' And he was right again, and under the loud applause I could sort of see another three men with beards, silent and dignified, and they all wore little gold ear-rings and big ruffs round their necks. And now we would really know whether Howard would make it or not, because everything depended on this last question, and if Howard got even one little bit of one part of it wrong, then it was good-bye to the money and welcome a lot of sneers and nastiness back in Bradcaster. Question No. 3 was this:

'The modern novel. Who were the authors of the following? *The Ambassadors; Where Angels Fear to Tread; The Good Soldier*.' And Howard said:

'Henry James; Edward Morgan Forster; Ford Madox Hueffer.' Then there was deathly silence, because Laddie didn't say, as he'd always said so far, 'And you're right.' Instead he sort of puzzled over his bit of paper and seemed to tremble a bit. He said, 'I'm terribly sorry, Howard, I'm really dreadfully sorry, because it's such a tiny mistake you've made –' The audience went 'Awwwww,' very loud. 'Such a tiny mistake,' said Laddie, louder. 'What I've got written down here is not Ford Madox Hueffer but Ford Madox Ford.'

'All right,' said Howard, 'Ford Madox Ford.'

'I'm really dreadfully sorry, Howard, but you've got no second chance. Your first answer is the answer you mean, I made that clear now, didn't I?' And you could see poor Laddie was about near tears, and I was ready to collapse into the floor, but I still had this confidence in Howard, Howard must be right and the paper must be wrong. Howard said:

'That's all right. He called himself Ford Madox Hueffer and then he changed his name to Ford Madox Ford. It's one and the same man, you see. You check that with anyone.' Then there was kind of chaos. You got the idea that people were wildly ringing people up on the phone, and that other people were wildly going through big books somewhere at the back of the studio, and meanwhile the organist, who I also met and I thought was not a very nice sort of a man, was playing sort of spooky music on his electric organ to fill up the time. There was real pandemonium too in the audience, and arguments were going on, and people kept patting me on the back and saying, 'There, there, girl.' But very soon there was Laddie receiving a bit of paper from Vicki, and he read it and then he looked overjoyed and then he cried out, very loud indeed, 'He's right, he's perfectly right! He's absolutely right, everybody!' Then he was dragging Howard out of the box and pumping his hand, and the two girls were kissing him, but I didn't mind, then before I knew where I was I was being pushed up on to the stage and facing the cameras and kissing Howard myself and seeing the cheque for one thousand pounds with my own eyes, and there were loud cheers and then the show was over. Howard said, hugging me, 'This is nothing, darling, nothing at all. This is just the beginning.' And then we were whirled off backstage for a drink.

# 9

WE GOT A train back to real London, and outside the station Howard called a taxi and we were taken to one of the really big hotels, right in the middle of London. It seemed like the world was at our feet, riding through the busy town with all lights around us, the taxi having to stop very often and get caught in traffic jams, though, but I didn't mind, I was in no hurry for anything, holding Howard's hand in the taxi as if it was our courting days all over again. London somehow seemed to have a special smell of its own, different from the smell of Bradcaster, a sort of smell of bigness, but it wasn't too big for either of us that night. We got to the hotel, which was a big giant of a place, with all lights inside it and people coming and going and the swing-doors never stopping swinging, and the commissionaire came to open the taxi door for us, and there was Howard giving out silver left and right. Then I remembered that we'd not brought any luggage with us. That was daft, and I couldn't help laughing a bit, though I also felt a bit ashamed. We'd left the house that morning, all dressed up, and we just hadn't thought of packing even a toothbrush. I suppose that was because of feeling free as the air, me anyway, having given up my job at the Supermarket, and even a toothbrush is something that makes you feel tied down. Howard had to laugh, too, because he hadn't thought either, and now we wondered what to do, all the shops being closed. We couldn't just go in and book a room for the night and not have any luggage, though at one point Howard said why not? The commissionaire was a very nice big man with a lot of medals and he became very interested in what Howard and I were talking and laughing about. He was a fatherly sort of a man. He said if we were in that position it did make it a bit awkward, people at the reception desk always fearing the worst and this was a respectable hotel. Then Howard explained who he was and the commissionaire said, 'I thought your face looked a bit familiar, sir. Last Thursday I was off ill, nothing serious, a bit of malaria I'd picked up in the first war, and I saw this programme on the telly, and, as I say, I can see now that you're the same gentleman. Well, sir, fancy that, winning a thousand nicker.' Both Howard and I had to smile at that word, it being a London word. 'Well, sir,' the commissionaire went on, 'the best thing is for you to tell the people at the desk who you are and how you didn't intend to stay the night and now that you've won you want to celebrate a bit and they won't think there's anything strange about it at all.' Howard said thank you and gave the commissionaire ten bob, and then we went in and over the deep burgundy-coloured carpet, with lights flashing all over the walls and the place full of very rich Jews and their wives, very well-dressed and talking with their hands a lot, and, smiling and laying on the charm, Howard explained to the smart young lady at the desk what the position was. She was a bit cold and polite, saying, 'Oh, yaas?' and 'Rahlly?' but the girl who was with her behind the desk, a very jolly-looking girl, said she knew who Howard was and wasn't it marvellous, and then everything was all right. As Howard said to me over and over later on, it wasn't a question of doing anything wrong coming to a posh hotel without luggage, it was a question of not doing anything *cheap*. It would have been all right just to pay in advance, as you usually have to if you bring no luggage, for some reason, but Howard didn't like anybody to get the wrong idea, and I agreed with him there.

Anyway, we went up to our room, and it was a very nice room, though little, with an electric fire, a radio, a dressing-table with strip-lighting, and even a place for plugging in an electric razor. When we'd freshened ourselves up a bit we realised how hungry we were, all the excitement and everything else making us forget it rather, and Howard said we wouldn't eat in the hotel but would take a taxi to some big restaurant and have a really good slap-up meal with champagne as well. So we went downstairs and the commissionaire was only too ready to call us a taxi and off we went to this big restaurant whose name I've forgotten. It was pretty full but we got bowed to a table and I had to hold back a fit of giggles for some reason, and when he was ordering some wine Howard gave me another of his surprises, but of course it was only his poor old photographic brain really. When the wine waiter came Howard said we'd have a bottle of champagne, I forget the name of it, a French name, but Howard had done French at the grammar school, and he said we'd have either 1953 or 1955, but no other year, whatever all that meant, though Howard explained to me later on that those were vintage years and some were good and some were bad but those two years were very good. I said I wouldn't know the difference, but he said that wasn't the point, he was determined to get the best this world could offer of everything for me, and for himself, in the short time that was left. I didn't get that about the short time that was left, but I thought that he must be referring to the H-Bomb or something or the Polaris missile or whatever it was he was always worrying about. Anyway, this champagne came along and Howard looked at the bottle and sure enough on the label it said 1957. 'That,' said Howard to the wine-waiter, 'is not what I asked for. What I asked for was either 1953 or 1955. If you haven't got either of those then I'm willing to take a 1952, but I'm not having this 1957, because 1957 was a lousy vintage year for champagne, and I'm just not having it, so there.' The wine-waiter sort of sneered and said:

'I assure you, sir, 1957 was an excellent year for champagne. One of the best.' Howard got very red and then said:

'I assure you that you're wrong. 1957 was a rotten year, one of the very worst. There've only been two years to touch it in living memory and those were 1939 and 1951, so take that bottle back and bring me what I asked for and don't be too long about it.'

Well, that certainly put him in his place, fat sneering man as he was, thinking perhaps we weren't good enough to come into his rotten old place. And though Howard said this place was supposed to have the best food in all London, I didn't think much of what I had, which was a piece of duck with orange sauce, the gravy being quite cold and the orange sauce very sour. I didn't think much to it at all, I'd rather have been at home with baked beans on toast in front of the fire with the telly going full blast, but Howard got very fierce and said that I'd *got* to have the very best and he'd make sure I got the very best even if it killed both of us. He grinned when he said that, so I didn't take him too seriously. After this duck of mine and Howard's what-was-called-tournedos, we had a chocolate mousse which was quite nice, and then Howard called for brandy and the wine-waiter, who must have been smarting a bit after Howard showed him that he knew what was what, said, 'What vintage year, sir?' Then Howard got so red in the face and clenched his teeth so much the wine-waiter decided that he hadn't been so funny after all, for he said. 'Just my little joke, sir,' and darted off to get some brandy. Of course, by this time, having had about half a bottle of champagne to myself, I was all giggly and even feeling a bit loving. But Howard talked quite seriously for a bit while we had our coffee and this brandy about what our plans were going to be. I let my attention wander a bit and looked round the room. There were some very chic women, but chic isn't everything and I didn't think one of them could touch me for Sheer Natural Unspoilt Beauty, as they call it, and I thought Howard was by far the handsomest man in that room. Howard was saying:

'A trip round the world, perhaps, or certainly a month or so in Jamaica or Bermuda or somewhere like that, then back home to Bradcaster for January 21st. That will suit us nicely.'

'That's my birthday,' I said.

'Yes,' Howard said, 'we'll celebrate your birthday at home.'

Then I said, 'A thousand pounds won't take us all that far, really, will it? And then there's the future. We neither of us have a job now. We'll have to start looking for something. It won't seem right, somehow, taking a holiday without having a job. I mean, you're supposed to be taking a holiday *from* something, aren't you?'

I must have been speaking loud, what with the champagne and the brandy, and, oh I forgot, a couple of gin-and-Italians to start off with, for Howard said, 'Shhhh.' So then I shut up and just giggled. But Howard said:

'This thousand pounds is just a beginning, see. It's something to be used. I'm going to turn it into, say, a hundred thousand, which is ten per cent of a million, and then that should be enough, I'd say.'

'Oh, Howard,' I said sternly, though I was still giggling, 'you're not going to do anything rash, are you? You're not going to gamble the money away, are you?'

'Don't worry,' said Howard, and he took my hand, which he said was a bit cold, into his two very hot hands, which were hot because of the heat in the place and the eating and drinking also. But if his were hot why were mine cold? Women are different from men. I said that aloud, a bit too loud, and giggled. Howard said, 'I'm going to take you back to the hotel now.'

'To bed,' I said, giggling a bit still.

'That's right,' he said, and there was a kind of bright sort of glitter in his eyes, sort of strong and triumphant. 'To bed.' As I've said before, Howard could be very very sweet. So he paid the bill, not tipping the wine-waiter, and we went off to bed.

WE GOT WOKEN up the next morning by the telephone ringing, and when Howard answered it he found it was somebody from the *Daily Window* who was downstairs in the entrance hall and would be glad if Howard could spare a few minutes for an interview. I suppose what had happened was that the commissionaire or the girls at the reception desk or somebody had earned an honest bob, which was perhaps what they did regularly, by letting the *Daily Window* know when there were people of interest or fame or something staying at the hotel. Of course, it would never be the really *big* people at this hotel, they always staying at places where you pay fifty pounds daily or more for a suite, only the small people, like those who'd won the pools and the telly quizzes and so on. Howard was a bit tired and a bit confused, I suppose, for he said, very meek, 'We'll be right down.' Actually, it was time we got up, for it was after ten, and we'd just slept like logs. It didn't take Howard as long to dress as it did me, so when he was ready he said, 'I'll be downstairs in that big lounge and I'll have coffee waiting for you.' That was sweet of him, always considerate.

My mouth felt awfully sour, and of course I had no tooth-brush, but I rubbed some soap round my teeth and was nearly sick, then swilled my mouth round and felt awful. But I was a brave girl and I dressed and made up and combed my hair carefully, put my coat on my arm and got the lift down. I was the only one in the lift going down from our floor, and the liftman was a foreigner and smelt like it, all garlicky, and he kept looking at me with eyes of Great Admiration, he even moaned a bit and went tlick tlick with his tongue just before stopping at a floor lower down and letting a fat rich couple in. I could tell now that I had a bit of a headache.

I walked into the lounge and could see Howard arguing away with a young man in a raincoat, and there were two silverish pots on the table, coffee and hot milk, and I was very glad to see that. The two stood up when I came and then sat down again and Howard was going for this young chap hammer and tongs. He seemed a nice young chap with wavy black hair thinning at the temples and sort of haunted eyes. He had an unhealthy look, what I can only call a London look, very pale and wan and as though he lived on sausage rolls from a canteen. I poured out coffee and drank some and felt tons better. Howard was saying:

'Our standards have gone all to hell, and it's newspapers like yours that are responsible. Pandering, that's all it is. Just appealing to the basest elements in all your readers.'

'Including yourself,' said the young man.

'Yes,' said Howard, 'I read it. Have you any objection?'

The young man smiled. You could see that Howard was all confused this morning and was contradicting himself. 'None at all,' said the young man. 'Only too pleased. Has it ever struck you that some people might buy it because they hate it? We don't mind why they buy it. I mean, our job is to sell it.'

'Debasement,' said Howard. 'Of the Queen's English, I mean. Full of "I guess" and "right now" and pandering to teenagers.'

'Teenagers have money,' said the young man. 'We give them what they want.'

'How do they know what they want? How does anybody know?' said Howard. 'If you just appeal to sex and easy sort of music and lyrics that'd make you want to puke and these kids clicking their fingers in a sort of stupid ecstasy, well then – What I mean is that you get so low it stands to reason you'll be appealing to the majority, the majority being stupid for the most part and just like animals.'

'This is a democracy,' said the young man. 'Sort of, that is. People are entitled to have what they want. What would

66

be better, do you think? Us educating them and telling them how to behave and what to think and all that, which is communist or fascist?'

'I should have thought you'd have had a duty,' said Howard, in his very stubborn way.

'We have a duty,' said the young man, 'and that is to give our readers what they want, that is to say what they pay for.'

'It's a lot of rubbish,' said Howard, mumbling. 'I only wish to God I could make myself clear.'

'You've made yourself clear,' said the young man. 'Now, what I really want to know is what you're going to do with the thousand pounds you've won.'

'I'm going to try to turn it into a hundred thousand,' said Howard. 'That's what I'm going to try and do.'

'Stock Exchange?' said the young man.

'No,' said Howard. 'Horses.' I didn't say anything, nor did the young man. 'It's the November Handicap on Saturday,' said Howard.

'Have you some special system?' asked the young man.

'Well,' said Howard, 'in a way. It's a question of using my photographic memory, if you see what I mean.'

'I don't quite,' said the young man. so Howard explained about his brain being able to take photographs and the young man listened with some interest, I thought. The young man said:

'I see. That explains a lot. I thought you were a student of literature. Somebody who loves books. I see now that you're not. Just a knack, that's all. A sort of trick. A kind of deformity, I suppose you could call it.' It looked as though he was now ready to attack Howard, Howard already having attacked him, or rather his newspaper. I poured out more coffee and then the pots were empty, so I smiled towards a waiter and he came like a shot to get more coffee. The young man was writing in his notebook. Howard said:

'I know, I know, I know,' getting louder each time. 'Don't you think I feel sick of the whole business? I'm just part of the whole rotten stinking nastiness. And last night, when I was answering those questions and getting them all right, I sort of had this feeling of being looked at from the grave. All those men looking at me, sort of sadly, sort of in sadness and pity. With their beards and their old-time costumes.' I nearly dropped my cup when Howard said that, because of course, as I mentioned, that sort of feeling came over me at the same time. That was telly-something (not television) I think you could call it, when two people are very close and can think the same thing at the same time. 'Humiliation,' said Howard. 'Humiliated at school when we had to do them, *The Mill on the Floss* and *A Shorter Boswell* and *Henry IV Part I* were our set books, and we drew dirty drawings all over them. And the teachers were no better than we were. And now humiliated by just being used to win a thousand pounds. And humiliated by you, too.' That didn't seem fair to me, for the young man had said nothing about these writers and poets. I noticed that he had a small blackhead over his lip, and perhaps he had nobody at home to see that he looked respectable before he came out in the morning. So I said:

'Are you married?'

'No, madam,' said the young man. And to Howard he said, 'If that's the way you feel, why don't you give the money away? Why don't you give it to some starving young poet or somebody?'

'I don't know any,' said Howard, a bit grumpy.

'I know several,' said the young man.

'Besides,' said Howard, 'my intention is to give more than money. Much more than money. I'll put things right for everybody. You just wait and see.'

Soon the young man left, saying he'd got to go to London Airport to meet somebody or other just arriving there, and then Howard said to me, 'We'd better get back to Bradcaster. It's the November Handicap tomorrow, and there's a lot to do.' I didn't say anything about that, Howard would always go his own way, but I did say I was hungry. So Howard rang up the station and found there was a train at 1.5, and then we went off to have a kind of mixed grill, which would do for both breakfast and lunch. I ate very heartily but Howard didn't eat much. He was deep in thought, poor Howard, so I left him to it. But I got through my own, which was a bit of steak and two sausages, a fried egg and tomatoes and fried potatoes, and I had a sausage of his, too. Then we went by tube to the station, the hotel bill of course having been paid, Howard looking a bit scruffy, not having shaved, and his collar showing the London dirt (London is really a filthy city, far worse than Bradcaster). At the station Howard bought magazines for me – *Womanly*, *Female* and *Mother and Child*, though why he bought the last one I don't know. For himself he bought the *Winning Post*, the *Racing Times* and a little book called *Cope's Racegoer's Encyclopaedia*. We got into a second-class compartment this time, like fools, for Howard had booked two first-class *returns*, not singles. It was force of habit, and Howard's photographic brain seemed to be very busy. We only woke up to our stupidity when the man came round, just before Crewe, to look at our tickets, and of course we had to move to a first-class carriage, though we were quite comfortable where we were. I don't mean we *had* to really, but it would have been a complete waste of money otherwise. And all the time, in second and first, Howard was going through his book and his papers, closing his eyes now and then, his lips moving away as if he was praying, but it was only the names of horses, as far as I could tell, anyway.

# II

WHEN WE GOT back home I got us something to eat and Howard made a fire, for it was perishing. And when we'd had our baked beans on toast and a pot of tea, then Howard said, 'I'm going to get down to it. It may fail, of course, but also it may succeed. If it doesn't succeed, what will you say?'

'I won't say anything,' I said. 'I leave it to you.' He kissed me for that. Then he closed his eyes as though he was in pain and began to recite names of horses. '1936, Newtown Ford. 1937, Solitaire. 1938, Pappageno. 1939, Tutor –' Those were all the winners of the Manchester Handicap. '1954, Abandoned. 1955, Tearaway. 1956, Trentham Boy. 1957, Chief Barker.' And I was checking these names with the book, and of course he was perfectly right. What I had to keep reminding myself was that this wasn't clever, it was just something that Howard had been born with. The young man from the *Daily Window* had called it a deformity, and that's really what it was. Howard said, 'Now I'll have a go at tomorrow's runners.' Then he went through the list in the paper and then he just knew them, just like that, for he was able to recite them straight off. Then he said, 'This is the hard part. What I have to imagine now is this *Cope's Racegoer's Encyclopaedia* for next year. What I have to close my eyes and see now is this page with all the winners for all the different years and this year's winner at the end of the list.'

'Oh, that's crazy,' I said. 'That's just absolutely mad.'

'It's all mad,' said Howard. 'All crazy and mad and all nasty. But it won't be for much longer.' Then he shut his eyes tight and sort of made a stab at it. 'No good,' he said. 'I just can't see anything.' And he tried all evening and he couldn't see anything All he could see was last year's winner at the bottom of the page, and he kept swearing, poor pet, because they wouldn't let him see this year's winner.

'Give it up for the time being,' I said. 'Give it a rest. Don't try forcing it. A man forced his pig and it died.'

'Forced it to do what?'

'I don't know. That's what they used to say. Come and have a look at the telly.' So I switched the TV on and we sat there watching, Howard very gloomy. There was an old film on that night, a very bad film about war in the desert, with men whistling *Lili Marlene* and tanks and antitank guns and Rommel, very dull and old-fashioned. I mean, we've got our own troubles without being reminded of all the troubles other people had in the past. 'El Alamein,' said Howard, loud, all of a sudden. 'That's it. That gives me the clue.' Then he switched the TV off, then stumbled to the switch of the light, and he said, 'Now I'm going to have a look,' so he shut his eyes so he could look all the better, then he said, 'It's all right. It's the winner.'

'Which one?' I asked.

'Dalnamein,' shouted Howard. 'I can see it here, clear as anything, all in plain black and white, at the bottom of the page. Dalnamein, it says. Ridden by J. Greenaway. Trained by –'

'Never mind about all that,' I said. 'How much are you going to put on?'

He opened his eyes and looked at me as if I was barmy. 'The lot,' he said. 'The whole thousand.'

'Will your bookie take that amount?'

'He'll take it,' said Howard. 'He'll only be too glad to. He'll spread it out, see, in case he loses. Which he will, of course. But he doesn't know it.' Then he started rustling newspapers all over the place, looking for the odds and whatnot. 'An outsider,' said Howard. 'That's what it is.'

'Oh, do be careful,' I said. I sort of pleaded. This was all too mad for words, this was. 'Don't put all that lot on. Put on half. Let's keep five hundred. It's a terrible risk.'

'Terrible risk nothing,' said Howard, loftily sort of. 'It's not our money, really. What I mean is, I don't really deserve

71

it. It's just this brain of mine. Now, if it had been some poor old professor all dressed in rags, a man who'd read all those books and knew all about it – But it was just my brain, not any trouble I'd taken really. If we lose, we lose. We won't have lost anything really.' There was no doing anything with poor Howard, he had to have his own way. He loved me dearly, as he showed and proved time and again, but he would have his own way about what he said he knew about, so I left it at that. After all, I could go back to the Supermarket tomorrow with no trouble at all, and Howard could get a job all right, especially now with him being well-known. He could even go on the stage as what they called a Memory Man. There was nothing to worry about really, but I couldn't help thinking what a waste it would be, all that money down the drain.

Next morning Howard went out early, with his best overcoat on. He didn't come back till about midday, but when he walked in he nodded sort of grimly and said, 'I had a bit of trouble, strange as it may seem, but it's all right now.' I said:

'So it's all on, is it?'

'Every penny.' And he nodded again. Well, that day I'd got some fish fingers for dinner, five each, and I'd made some chips, but neither of us could eat much. At one point in the meal Howard suddenly shut his eyes and said, 'I *think* it says Dalnamein.'

'Too late now,' I said. And I made some tea, very strong. The race was at 1.55 and of course it was on the TV, so at about 1.30 we were sitting down in front of it, our hearts going like mad, and I asked, 'What odds did you get?'

'Twenty-eight to one,' said Howard. £29,000, I thought to myself. It was too much for people like us, and I felt a bit better about not winning, being sure now that Howard had done the wrong thing and he himself not too happy, as you could tell, him drawing on cigarettes, one after another, in a thirsty sort of way. And all the time the voice of the commentator at the race course was droning on about this horse and that horse, and they all looked alike to me. There was this seventeen-inch screen of ours, blobbing and snowing away with the cars passing outside, all full of horses neighing

72

and trotting or something, all to and fro. 'There it is,' said Howard in a gloomy way. 'That black sort of horse there. That's Dalnamein. I hope to God I've done the right thing.' And he began to bite his nails, a habit I've always hated, so I hit his fingers down from his mouth. He mumbled something and then the horses were all under starter's orders and then they were off. The commentator was telling us all about it in a voice like the voice of some parson in church, though very fast, all on the same note: 'And he so-and-so so-and-so so-and-so so-and-so's. And he so-and-so so-and-so so-and-so so-and-so's,' taking a big breath before each new 'and', and getting very excited. What happened was that New Warrior was in front with Mossy Face, Pandofell, Sunrise and Sabot behind, and Windy-edge one of the backmarkers, whatever that meant. With seven furlongs to go Bonnie Brae got ahead of New Warrior, Sunrise, Prime Mover and Sabot. Then it was the final turn and Prime Mover got a slight advantage and then Pandofell moved up and there were two furlongs to go and Pandofell was a length in front.

'Come on, Dalnamein!' yelled out Howard all of a sudden, and we were both banging our fists on our knees and the commentator was going at it very fast on this one note, and 'Come on, Dalnamein, you bastard!' yelled out Howard. Dalnamein was challenging and Windy-edge was coming up and they were into the final furlong and Dalnamein had taken the lead and was holding on and it was Windy-edge just behind and Dalnamein held on and then there was the winning post and Dalnamein had beaten Windy-edge by a neck, as they call it, and Howard and I didn't know whether to jump in the air and smash all the furniture or just pass out, sort of numb. What I said was: 'I think I'll go and make a cup of tea.' And I went off and did it and Howard switched the telly off and just sat there looking at its big square creamy eye which was blind, with his mouth open. While we were sipping the tea, and believe me we felt that we needed it, Howard said, 'Twenty-eight thousand pounds, that will be. What I'll do is to put half of that in the bank for the time being and I'll play the other half for a week, say, and with a bit of luck we'll have enough to do what we're going to.'

'You get a thousand back,' I said. 'That's your stake money. The bookie gives you that back, you see.'

'Oh, yes,' said Howard, 'I know all about that, but that'll be the thousand I got for seeming to know all about books and all that sort of thing, and I shall give that away.'

'Who to?' I asked, being past being surprised by anything Howard could do or say.

'Oh, I'll send it to that young fellow from the *Daily Window*. He said he knew a lot of writers and poets and suchlike who are half-starved. That's the least I can do.'

'You'll do nothing of the sort,' I said, nastily, a bit. 'He never put anything in the paper about you. He did nothing for you.'

'It's not for him,' said Howard. 'It's for some poet who's living in an attic, writing his poetry that nobody wants, starving.'

'How do you know you could trust him to give the money to somebody who deserves it?'

'He seemed a decent honest young fellow. He gave me his card, see.' And Howard took a card out of his pocket with *Albert Reeves, Daily Window* printed on it. 'I mean,' said Howard, 'it's only fair, isn't it? It's sort of a way of paying back all those dead old poets and writers and suchlike, that neither of us have even read. It's the least I can do. I'll feel freer that way, if you see what I mean. Under no more obligation.'

There was no point in me saying anything more, and, anyway, there we were quarrelling about a mere measly thousand quid when we'd got more money than we knew what to do with, me anyway, and Howard talked about making yet more money. It was best for me to give up arguing and thinking and planning and do something about getting our tea ready. Not just a cup of tea, of course, but something cooked, those fish fingers that we hadn't been able to eat warmed up and with a drop of tomato ketchup on them. That would do all right for tea.

## 12

THE NEXT WEEK, as you can well imagine, was a pretty busy one, starting with Sunday when, of course, we had to go and see my Mum and Pop and tell them we'd give them a present, anything they'd like for the house, and they thought they'd have a refrigerator, so we said we'd see about that for them. That was in the morning. In the afternoon Howard went to see his auntie, just on his own, and I've no idea what he did for her, but I should imagine he gave her a cheque, though for what amount I've no idea and I didn't ask. I could see now the point of having a bank account, Howard having opened one a year or two back but we never having anything in it till now, really. I used to say, 'The wages come in and we spend the wages. And here you are paying out bank charges and whatnot and the bank doing nothing to earn them.' But he always said, 'It's the done thing. Besides, one of these days we'll really be needing a bank, you mark my words.' I never dreamed, of course, of what would really happen, but here it was, large as life and twice as beautiful, and Howard as usual was right.

On Sunday evening Myrtle and her husband Michael came round, and of course Howard could see what they were after as much as I could, for all Howard being absorbed in racing papers and what to back on next week's races. Myrtle was saying how marvellous it all was, gushing, and of course we didn't breathe a word of what Howard had already made out of the thousand quid, any more than we had done to Mum and Pop and Howard's auntie, though them we thought we *would* tell later, when Howard had finished what he called his plan. Myrtle and Michael were only the start really of people who didn't usually call on us starting to call on us and we got a bit fed up with it, although Howard said, 'All this was to be expected. This is human nature, this is.' There were the Ogdens, Maisie Bowyer who was divorced, Jack Braintree, Liz Bamber and her husband-to-be, and lots of others, all cadging in a polite way, but all we gave them was a cup of tea and a ginger biscuit.

On Monday morning Howard wrote a letter to this young chap on the *Daily Window*, telling him he was enclosing crossed cheque for £1,000 to be used to help starving poets and suchlike, but there was to be no publicity of any sort. Howard said he felt better after that, and he said the ghosts of those dead writers and poets who he had shamefully exploited (his words) could now sleep in peace. Oh, Howard was a funny boy, but you could see what he was getting at in a sort of way. Then he got down to putting money on the horses, though it was a matter now of opening up accounts with other bookies in the town, George Welbeck ('Welbeck Never Welshes') obviously not going to be too pleased with Howard after the November Handicap, though if they don't like their customers winning why do they go into business at all? Anyway, that suddenly made me think of something that Howard hadn't thought of, and I said to him, 'You haven't got the money from Welbeck yet. And here you are sending off cheques for a thousand quid all over the place. Aren't you being a bit previous?' He winked at me and said, 'Settling-up day's next Saturday. I've postdated this cheque, see.' I shook my head, not quite knowing what that word meant, but I left it all to Howard, as usual. Howard always knew best, poor boy. So Monday morning was a busy morning for him, going to the other turf commission agents in Bradcaster and opening up accounts with them. And now I'll tell you what horses he backed and in what races and how much he won altogether, as well as I can remember, that is. I never asked him what method he used, but I know it wasn't the November Handicap one, because these small races would not be in Cope's Book. He might have used a pin for all I know or got inside information or something, for he was out all day, only coming home about five and then having a rosy sort of look about him. If he'd been drinking, I just don't know where, and he was certainly never offensive, just more loving than usual if that was possible.

Well, on Monday there was racing at Birmingham, and Howard came unstuck in the one o'clock, backing Noble Warrior for a win and it came in fourth and there were only four runners. But in the one-thirty he backed Cobbity each way, and that came in third at 100–9. In the two o'clock he backed Ladignac each way, and that was 33–1 and came in second. In the two-thirty he backed Up the Vale for a win and it came in third. But in the three o'clock Howard did really well. He backed Winter Wanton and Hydrant each way (and he had a lot on, how much exactly he never told me, but it must have been a lot) and Winter Wanton came in first at 6–1 and Hydrant third at 8–1. It was a very big field, too. And in the three-thirty he backed Eire's Flame each way, and that came in third at 33–1, ridden by T. Brookshaw. When he came home I asked him how much he reckoned he'd won (or lost, because I didn't know how much the stakes were) on the day, and he did a very funny drunken sort of thing. He put his finger by the side of his nose, swaying a bit. So I gave him his tea (tinned kidneys in gravy with mashed potatoes) and didn't ask any more, and he was off to bed at half-past eight, snoring away.

Now next day Howard didn't back anything, I don't know why, because there was big racing at Birmingham, I knew that much. But he had some queer system of his own. On the Wednesday there was small sort of racing at Worcester with heavy going, and Howard backed Just My Mark each way in the one o'clock and it came in second at 100–7. In the one-thirty he backed the winner – Lynnmoor at very poor odds of 5–2, but he said that, altogether, he'd bet about six hundred quid on that all told, so it was a nice little win. That gave me an idea how big the stakes were, but I didn't worry, because we had fourteen thousand nicely tucked away, unless George Welbeck who never welshed decided to welsh. But Welbeck was too big a man for that, and a big bookie never loses, nor welshes either, and George Welbeck's motto was really the motto he'd used when he first started in business in a very small way. So the money was quite safe, and we'd never in all our lives ever dreamed of having so much money. Anyway, in the two o'clock at Worcester Soltown came last, and Howard had backed that for a win. But he backed the favourite in the two-thirty, which was Spring Bird ridden by S. Mellor, and the odds were 5–2. His luck seemed to be in now, because he also got the winner in the three o'clock, Wire Warrior at 100–9, and Brooksby Boy came in second in the three-thirty at 20–1, and all Howard would say about that was that he had a 'packet' on it.

Howard did nothing on the Thursday, concentrating everything, as he put it, on the Friday and Saturday of that week, and on the Friday there was racing at Sandown. Dargent came first in the one o'clock at 20–1, and Howard cursed because he hadn't put enough on it. Then he had no further wins or places until the two-thirty when Cannobie Lee came in third at 6–1 and he cursed again about Flame Gun, first at 100–9, which he'd very nearly backed. But he had no real cause to curse or grumble, because he cleaned up a nice little packet, as he called it, on Silver Dome, which came first at 20–1 in the three o'clock. On Saturday morning letters came for Howard, and they all had cheques in them, and the only one he'd show me was the one from George Welbeck, and you could hardly believe your eyes. £29,000, clear as daylight. Howard looked at the other cheques and said, 'Quite satisfactory, but we haven't finished yet.' And then, when he'd had his breakfast, which was a bit late, this being Saturday, he went off in his best overcoat to the bank.

He didn't come back till dinner-time, and, knowing there was big racing at Sandown Park, Newcastle and Doncaster that afternoon and that this was Howard's last day for backing horses, I didn't put much in the way of dinner, just a tin of salmon with mashed potatoes, but neither of us could eat much, just like the previous Saturday, only, of course, not quite so bad. They were showing some of this racing on the TV, but Howard said he didn't want to watch it, it took too much out of you, and he'd be quite content to hear the results later on the wireless. He said he'd go to bed and come down when the sports news came on. I don't know why it is, but the little march tune they have on the wireless when the sports news is coming is one of the saddest little tunes in the world to my ears. I wonder why that should be? There's something somehow very miserable about five o'clock on a Saturday in winter and I can't explain it. But when Howard came down to hear the racing results there was not much misery, I can tell you. He'd gone down a bit on some of the races, but in the three o'clock at Sandown he'd backed Sabre, which came in first at 100–9. At Newcastle, in the Medburn Novices' Hurdle, Venturesome Warrior came in second at 13–2, and Howard had backed that each way. In the Alnwick Castle Hurdle he got the winner, John D, at 20–1, but after that no more luck at Newcastle. But it was at Doncaster that Howard did best, what with Royal Spray winning in the one o'clock at 100–7, and Nigarda second in the Try Again Hurdle at three o'clock, 11–2, and Pendle Pearl, 33–1, in the same race coming third. So that was that. 'Well,' said Howard.

'How do we stand, love?' I asked.

'I'll work it all out,' he said, 'when I've had my tea.'

'Tea won't be ready for a bit,' I said. 'I've made some fishcakes out of the tinned salmon and the mashed potatoes we left, and those will have to be fried.'

'All right,' he said. 'I'll work it out roughly now while you're getting the tea ready.' So I went off to the kitchen to fry the fishcakes, not really thinking about anything really, being a bit numb as far as the money was concerned and not really able to take it all in. While I was setting the table Howard was in his fireside chair with his attaché case on his knee as a sort of desk, working out his winnings on a bit of paper. His lips were moving and he was frowning a bit, but I said nothing. When I brought the fishcakes and the teapot in and said, 'Tea up, love,' he said, 'Just a minute.' So I sat down and started buttering a slice of bread and then I poured some OK sauce on my fishcakes (two each) and then Howard said:

'I make it, but this is only rough, mind, I make it, and I may have made one or two mistakes, but I make it, including what I paid in the bank this morning, I make it –'

'Come on,' I said.

'I make it,' said Howard, 'just under eighty thousand. Just under eighty thousand quid, that is.' And he frowned.

'Oh, Howard,' I said, my mouth open and showing what I was eating, and looking at him as though he'd done something wrong, 'Oh, Howard.'

'Call it seventy-nine thousand odd,' said Howard, 'just to be on the safe side.' He nodded a bit, still frowning. 'I reckoned on about a hundred thousand, but I suppose this might as well do.'

'Oh, Howard,' I said again. I didn't seem capable of saying anything else. Then I said, 'Come and get your tea.'

'Of course,' he said, 'if you'd like me to take it up to the hundred thousand mark, it wouldn't be any trouble.'

'Don't tempt providence,' I said. 'Seventy-nine thousand is a terrible lot of money. A wicked lot of money. What are we going to do with it all?'

'We're going to spend it,' said Howard. Then he sat down to his tea. 'These look to be nice fishcakes,' he said.

# 13

I WON'T GO into all the details of arguing and planning and suggesting and quarrelling and lying awake in bed and then sleeping and tossing and turning so that the clothes fell off and we kept waking up again, cold, and all the cigarettes we smoked, more than I ever smoked in my life before, and the bottles that Howard had on the sideboard – Grand Marnier, Dubonnet, Invalid Port, Spanish Sherry and the like – from which we drank, so that now I was richer than I'd ever been in my life I was also iller than I'd ever been in my life. I kept urging Howard that we'd got to be sensible and put some of this money by for a rainy day and he said all right, but in a half-hearted and sly sort of way. He said:

'There's one thing, anyway. Will you agree that it would be a good idea for us to take a bit of a holiday and get somewhere a bit nearer the sun than England, this being likely to be a perishing sort of winter?'

'Well,' I said, 'there's Christmas coming, isn't there? It's not right to go on our holidays over Christmas, is it? I've never heard of anybody doing that sort of thing before. Not people of our class, anyway.' And in my mind I could see all the shops lit up and the children with their balloons and the lovely cold warm smell of Christmas and us away from it. Howard got in a rage and said:

'Our class? People of our class? We're not the class we used to be, my girl, nor nothing like it. We're what is known as the moneyed classes now, and we shall behave as such if it's the last thing we do.' Then he got a bit gentler and said that we could have a lovely Christmas away from Bradcaster, just the two of us, with the loveliest presents in the world and champagne and dancing under a tropical moon and stars and the palm-trees swaying in the scented breeze, a very romantic idea, like the pictures in the days when there was that sort of picture and people used to go to the pictures. But I said:

'Christmas isn't right in a hot place. It just can't be Christmas at all, can it? I mean, it stands to reason that Christmas has got to be *cold*, doesn't it?' And then Howard went on with his photographic brain about the day temperature in Bethlehem when Jesus was born and that I was being conservative or conventional or something. So I said Christmas wouldn't be Christmas without it being cold, over and over again, till Howard very nearly gave in completely. What we decided at the finish was that we should take a trip to America, in a plane, and be in some big hotel or somewhere in New York for Christmas, and then after Christmas we'd fly or sail or something to the Caribbean. Howard drew me on a piece of paper a perfect drawing of America with all the islands, straight out of his photographic head, and he showed me what was meant by the Caribbean, which I'd never properly understood before.

Well, it wasn't just a question, like on the pictures, of ringing up the airport and asking if there was a plane for New York and being told 'Yes, sir, leaving in thirty minutes, you'll just make it.' It was a lot more trouble than that for people of our class. In the first place, we had to have passports and that took some time. Then there was arranging things with the travel agents in Bradcaster High Street, Jepson's World Travel, which I'd passed a hundred times and never been inside. It was exciting, looking at all the folders with pictures of absolutely red men and women in sunglasses lying on tropical beaches, absolutely yellow, and all the pictures showing bridges like Meccano sets and old cathedrals and skyscrapers. I left everything to Howard and all that Howard left to me was going to buy clothes for myself, Bradcaster being a very good shopping centre with three big stores as good as anything you get in London, and very good for clothes. What Howard did was to give me a whole cheque-book that was blank except for where he'd signed his name, and what I had to do was to fill in the amount I was paying in each of the stores and then they'd send what I'd bought as soon as the cheque cleared, whatever that means. Well, I had a marvellous time, as you can guess. I bought cocktail dresses and costumes and playsuits and stockings and shoes and underwear. Also handbags and three lovely evening dresses, all frothy and plunging. When I met Howard again, who'd also been doing some shopping, but for himself, I told him what I'd bought and they'd be sending it all on, and he said:

'Where's your mink coat?'

I looked at him with my mouth open a bit, 'But that's impossible,' I said. 'A mink coat costs thousands and thousands. A mink coat isn't for people like me.' Howard nearly went mad and hit me on the street and said:

'It is, it is, it is. You're to get a mink coat, do you hear? One that costs thousands and thousands. Do you hear?' And he sort of did a dance of rage in the street so that people turned and looked at him. So I went to Einstein's the furriers and they got the shock of their life when I said I wanted a mink coat, full-length, like what the Queen wears. That woke them up, I can tell you, so that they spilled their tea and one girl knocked her cup over. They even brought a little man up from the cold storage, a nice little Jewish man with rings and curly hair where he wasn't bald and he bowed round me and couldn't do enough. It ended up with them not having a good enough one in stock and they'd ring up their branch in London and they'd only be too pleased to come to our house and let me try several on. So I was bowed off the premises in great excitement.

Now when we got home from a day's shopping about four in the afternoon one day we found a man waiting on the doorstep. We couldn't see him very clearly, but he said, 'Mr Shirley? Is it Mr Shirley, patron of the arts?' Howard couldn't make much of this, so he said, 'Just a minute' and then opened the front door. 'What's all this about?' he asked. 'You'd better come in.' Well, this man came in and we could see him clearly now in the light in the hallway. He was a young man with a bitter sort of face, no overcoat on but a thick pullover up to his neck, so I suppose he had no

83

shirt on either. He was a dark young man with dark rings under his eyes and a droopy sort of a mouth. His hair wasn't exactly long but he had a long straight bit in front that kept falling into his eyes. His complexion was very sallow, rather dirty-looking. But he had a very sweet smile. He wore a pair of flannel trousers that looked to me to be too thin for the winter and moreover were very dirty and stained and his shoes were dirty too. 'Now then,' said Howard, taking this young man into the living-room, 'what is it you've come to see about?' For Howard thought it might be somebody from the travel agency or one of the shops.

'I wanted to say that you did the right thing with your money, Mr Shirley,' said the young man. 'I got it yesterday. Nine hundred pounds. I promise you I won't let you down.'

'Nine hundred?' said Howard, puzzled. 'Oh, I see. But,' he said, puzzled again, 'what I sent was a cheque for a thousand.'

'Bert Reeves kept a hundred for himself,' said the young man. 'He said he'd really acted as an agent and he'd kept ten per cent as commission. Oh, my name, by the way, is Redvers Glass.'

Howard had to get him to say that name over and over again until he'd got it. It was a queer sort of name, I thought, but there was no real reason why it shouldn't be a real name. 'Well,' said Howard, 'it was very kind of you to come and say thank you in person, so to speak.'

'Not *so to speak*,' said this Redvers Glass. 'It is really me in person.' That, I thought, was a bit rude, but Redvers Glass said it with a nice smile so you couldn't take offence. 'I'm writing the story of my life,' he said. 'In verse. That nine hundred pounds will come in very nicely.'

'I'm very glad,' said Howard. 'Look, you needn't have come all this way just to say thank you, you know. You could have just sent a letter or something.'

'I thought,' said Redvers Glass, and the silly thing was that we were all standing up in the living-room, Howard and me still with our coats on, 'I thought I'd come and actually see with my own eyes somebody who is a patron of the arts. And,' he said, looking round, 'lives in a council house. With,' he said, suddenly turning towards me, 'a most charming wife, if, of course, it is your wife.'

'Look here,' said Howard, ready to get nasty.

'What I mean,' said this Redvers Glass, 'was that she might be your sister or your betrothed or something like that.' Then he sort of bowed and grinned all round and I had to giggle a bit.

'What train did you think of catching?' said Howard. 'I suppose you'll want to get back to London fairly soon.'

'London?' said Redvers Glass, as though London was a dirty habit or something. 'Oh, no, not London. If the provinces can have patrons of the arts the provinces is where I ought to be. If Bradcaster can produce men like you, unselfish givers to the cause, Bradcaster is the sort of place I've long been looking for. Nobody in London has ever helped, no, nobody, no, not anybody at all.' And he grinned at me again. He must have been about Howard's own age.

'Bradcaster's all right,' said Howard. 'There's nothing much wrong with Bradcaster. You could do worse than stay in Bradcaster for a bit.' He kept eyeing Redvers Glass all the time, sort of weighing him up. 'There's one or two good hotels in Bradcaster, the Royal, the George, the Swinging Lamp.'

'The Swinging what?'

'The Swinging Lamp. And there's the White Lion which is a four-star place.'

'People like me don't stay in hotels,' said Redvers Glass, and he sort of hunched himself up, as if to make himself look very cold and small. 'People of my class. Perhaps people of your class stay in hotels, but me and my kind, no.' And he turned towards me, shaking his head very fast and going prrrrr with his lips. So I said:

'Well, we'd all better have a cup of tea. It's a perishing day.' And I went off to make it. Redvers Glass said:

'Very strong, please. I like it very strong.' I said:

'You'll get it the way I like it. Cheek.' But I couldn't help grinning a bit to myself as I went into the kitchen. You didn't often see people like this Redvers Glass in Bradcaster. You didn't often see poets and suchlike. While the kettle was boiling I put some biscuits on a plate and also took out of its tin the walnut cake which I'd bought a week before but neither Howard nor me had liked much, and then I made the tea and brought everything into the living-room. Howard was just saying to this Redvers Glass, 'You're a bloody impostor, that's what you are, and I've a damned good mind to chuck you out into the street!' When he saw me, Howard said, 'This man say's he's a writer and a poet and I asked him to recite me something he'd written just to see if he was genuine, and what he recited wasn't his own at all. It was part of 'To his Coy Mistress' by Andrew Marvell, 1621–78. He thought I wouldn't know, he thinks we're all bloody morons up here.' Redvers Glass grinned at me and gave me a wink while Howard was going on at him and then he said:

'That was just to test you.'

'It's not up to you to test me,' shouted Howard. 'It's up to me to test you, thank you very much.'

'Not at all,' said Redvers Glass. 'That looks delicious walnut cake. Please give me a really big slice.' I was only too glad to, because Howard didn't like it a bit and I wasn't all that keen. So Redvers Glass stuffed his mouth full of walnut cake and said something like 'Munch munch munch' to Howard. Then he swallowed and said, 'You're one of the very few men I've ever met who've been able to see through my little deception. You'd be surprised, really. Now I'll *really* recite you something of my own.' But to stop him doing that I said, 'Have some more walnut cake,' which he did, a bigger slice than before. He was very hungry. They never taught us at school to really appreciate poetry. This Redvers Glass seemed half-starved. He finished the whole walnut cake off with no trouble at all.

## 14

IT WAS QUITE a bit of a job getting rid of this Redvers Glass,
though it was more Howard wanting to get rid of him than
me. I'd often heard about poets, though not much at school,
and it was a really new experience for me to have one there in
our living-room. He was not very well-dressed, as I've already
said, but you could see he had something about him, especially
when he talked, and he had a nice voice, all fruity. He kept
on talking and telling us how he'd been at Oxford with this
Reeves man of the *Daily Window* and how Reeves had been
poor in those days and Redvers Glass's family had been very
rich, though now they had thrown him out or something for
being a poet and not wanting to go into the family business
or something. Anyway, at Oxford College or University or
whatever it's called, Redvers Glass had helped Albert Reeves
with money and Reeves had never been able to pay him back
but had always sworn that he would some day and here he'd
done it, in a way. That was Redvers Glass's story. He also
finished off the biscuits as well as the walnut cake and drank
six cups of tea, the last cup being almost pure water. So I asked
him if he'd like a drink from one of our bottles, which I could
see him eyeing in a thirsty sort of a way, and he said yes, so I
poured him out this Grand Marnier in mistake for sherry, but
he drank it without turning a hair. Then he wanted more and
wanted to start reciting his poetry, but Howard said, 'You get
off into town now and get a hotel for the night and then decide
what you want to do tomorrow.' Redvers Glass said:
  'London is finished, finished and finished and finished.' You
could tell that was the Grand Marnier coming out. 'The future
of healthy English art lies in the provinces. Yes, oh yes, that is

where the poet and musician will best flourish.' And a lot more like that, saying London was too big to care about anyone, and it had no heart, but in the provinces things were different. I didn't follow much of what he said, but I couldn't help the odd sly giggle. Anyway, Howard more or less threw him out and you could hear him singing a bit down the street, a real happy poet, as he should be with nine hundred quid of Howard's in his pocket or bank or wherever he had it. Then I giggled really out loud and Howard couldn't help smiling either. I got our supper ready now and, as we were in the money, I'd bought some tinned Russian Crab which was very expensive just about then because of the trouble or something, and we had it with vinegar and tinned potato salad and I'd made more tea. And after supper we didn't watch the TV. Instead we had a look at maps and things and talked about what we'd do when we got on our holiday, and we also read some of the letters that had come that day, begging letters from people in the town, so you could see somebody had been talking, somebody in the bank or at the bookie's office, but we burned all the letters when we'd read them, nobody really being deserving.

It was about half-past ten that we heard a loud knocking at our door. Howard went, of course. I didn't like that loud knocking, it being as though the loudness meant something horrid like somebody dying or very ill. I heard voices so I went out into the hall and on the doorstep was a policeman we didn't know, a big gormless copper with a very uneducated voice, and this copper had hold of this poet, Redvers Glass. Redvers Glass was very drunk, you could see that, so Howard did the right thing and asked the policeman to bring him into the hall, us not wanting passers-by or neighbours taking the dog for a walk to see all this. So Redvers Glass was dragged in by his scruff practically and propped up against the wall and I wanted to giggle very badly but I kept a straight face. The copper said:

'He were found drunk and incapable just by the Swingin' Lamp.' And Redvers Glass began to sing in a drunken way with his eyes shut a very rude song about the Street of a Thousand Somethings by the Sign of the Swinging Something Else. 'All we found in his pockets,' said the copper, 'by way of identificairshun were his cheque-book and a lot of five-quid notes and your address writ down on a bit of pairper, so it were thought best to bring him here.' And he looked very sternly at Howard as though it was all Howard's fault, which in a way I suppose it was. 'Perhaps he's some relairshun of yours,' said the policeman, 'though he don't talk like a Bradcaster chap.' Howard said:

'Why didn't you let him sleep it off in the cells? He's nothing to do with us. I just gave him some money, that's all.'

'Well,' said the copper, 'you can see what he's done with the money, can't you?' And he gave Howard another stern look and then a pitying and disgusted look sort of at Redvers Glass. Redvers Glass was still against the wall with his eyes shut burbling away at sort of poetry. You could just hear a few words coming out, making no sense at all, and then I realised that Redvers Glass was in the same position as we'd been that night in London, having no luggage and perhaps going from hotel to hotel and getting told there was no room and then going to get drunk. Really, in a way, he'd been very decent, not just coming back to us cadging a room for the night from us but trying to work things out for himself, a bit difficult, him being a stranger. Then Redvers Glass, still standing against the wall swaying, started to go straight off to sleep, snoring a bit. The copper said, 'You'd best give him a bed for the night, you being the only folks he knows in Bradcaster, and then he'd best get on his way in the morning. Daft young fool,' he said. Redvers Glass said:

'I heard that. I heard what you said. Won't have anybody calling me names,' and then he started to snore again.

'All right,' said Howard. 'Let's put him in the spare room. He shouldn't have done it. Taking advantage, really, that's what it was.' Well, the policeman just swung Redvers Glass over his shoulder in what's called the Fireman's Lift, but he could see our stairs were too narrow, so then he and Howard took one end of Redvers Glass each and sort of worked their way up the stairs with Redvers Glass's arms flopping at the sides and his mouth open and his eyes shut and still snoring away. It was very funny when you came to think of it, and I had to fight to keep down my giggling. I stayed downstairs, and I could hear crashes and bangs as they dragged him into the spare bedroom (where Myrtle had slept that time) and then a sort of big flop and heavy sighs and what sounded like Howard and the policeman wiping their hands as though what they'd carried upstairs was something wet. You could hear the flip flop of one hand wiping against the other. Then they came downstairs and the copper said again, 'Daft young fool.'

'He'll be all right in the morning,' said Howard. 'We'll dose him up with black coffee and then send him on his way. He's a poet, you see.'

'Ah,' said the policeman, nodding, as if that explained everything. 'Right. Well, much obliged to both of you,' and he shook hands with us in a very solemn way and said he'd got to be getting back to the stairshun. He spoke very broad. Just before going out he sort of grinned for the first time and said, 'He's a paw it and don't knaw it, got a bald ead and frightened to shaw it.' That was his bit of humour. Then he went off back to the station.

When we went to bed, which we did shortly after, it having been a very hard day, we could hear Redvers Glass snoring away, lying on his back which is what makes you snore, as well as too much drink. But it was a regular sort of snore, not jerky like my Pop's used to be, and you can sleep through that without too much trouble. These days, I ought to mention, Howard had quietened down a lot at night, and there was very little of this walking round the house in his sleep and putting the lights on and very little too of his talking and shouting out. He'd pretty well stopped doing all that at the time when he was getting ready for the quiz, as though his brain had too much to think about to bother with all that fun and games of the night. Only now and again he'd suddenly shout out the name of some book, as I took it to be, or some writer, or some date or other, but he very rarely got up these nights now. So I was getting more rest. And if I could sleep through the fear of Howard suddenly shouting out in my earhole, well, I could certainly sleep through all this snoring of Redvers Glass next door.

In the morning, which was cold and very dull, being nearly the end of November, Howard and I got up at the usual time of half-past seven, and we could still hear Redvers Glass honking away there next door while we were getting washed and dressed, and also while we were having breakfast of bacon and tomatoes in the living-room. We put on the wireless and had music and the news, and the snoring still went on and could be clearly heard above the radio and when the news came on these snores were a bit like a commentary and I couldn't help giggling a bit. It was a bit like this:

'Mr Gaitskell HONK said yesterday HONK he had every confidence that the Labour Party HONK would something-or-other HONK before the next election HONK.'

We had tea with our breakfast but Howard said I'd better make some really very strong coffee and then this Redvers Glass had better wake up and drink it and put himself right for his journey to wherever he was going. I said to Howard that Redvers Glass had said that he was determined to stay here in Bradcaster, but Howard said nonsense, London was his place and that's where he was to go back to. Very stern, looking over the top of his newspaper. Well, it was nine o'clock and there was Redvers Glass still snoring away, and Housewives' Choice came on with Mrs Hoskins asks for the Sheep May Safely Graze Cha-cha-cha for her daughter-in-law in St Helens, and the honks came in nicely with the cha-cha-cha bits. I made this very strong coffee, expense being no object, and Howard said he'd take it up, which he did. But he seemed to have a lot of trouble waking up Redvers Glass the poet. I could hear 'Come on now, blast you,' and 'Huh? Huh?' and it seemed very amusing to me, I don't really know why. I suppose really it was something new in my life. Howard came downstairs frowning, not really having much of a sense of humour, and said, 'I've got him to wake up, that's one thing. The best thing is to leave him with that pot of coffee up there and let him come to, so to speak, gradually. Then he can have a shave with my razor, then he can go.' And he sat down, very stern again, to have a read of his paper.

Now what happened after this I get very confused about, as if I don't quite want to remember and my brain says, 'All right, love, you shan't remember if you don't want to.' The wireless was still on with Housewives' Choice, I do remember that, not yet having reached Five to Ten, which was a very short religious programme about a saint called Quentin Hogg or some such name. Howard put his paper down and said, 'I shall go upstairs now and have a shave and a bath and perhaps by the time I've finished, this one'll be ready to get ready and get out.' And Howard marched upstairs. Now that was one thing that struck me as silly, and showed that Howard's brain couldn't work like any ordinary man's, and that was that he'd had a wash and got properly dressed before breakfast, and he must have known that after breakfast he'd want to have a bath, having to get undressed, of course, to have it, and why did he take the trouble to get properly dressed before breakfast? It might have been the force of habit of going to work and only having a bath at week-ends except in summer, but still you'd think he might have *thought*. Anyway, he was up there in the bathroom, first having gone in to see how Redvers Glass was getting on, and from the mutterings you could tell that Redvers Glass was awake now though still in bed, and then the bathroom door clicked shut and the water was thudding away into the bath and Howard was sort of singing. We got our hot water, by the way, from an immersion heater which was already in the house and they had them in all the houses in our street.

I told myself that I'd better go upstairs and bring down the coffee-pot and cup and saucer (no sugar or milk) that were in Redvers Glass's room, as I'd finished the other washing-up and I didn't want to waste the sudsy water still in the bowl (Fairy Liquid, just a squeeze), so I went up, the whole house being full of the noise of Howard's bath and his singing. I went into the spare room with a sort of bit of excitement, and there was Redvers Glass lying in bed with his eyes open and very bright his eyes were. He had a bit of a beard and his hair was all over the place and he seemed to be in the nude. When he saw me it was like a fever in his eyes and my heart sort of beat pretty fast. 'Quick,' he said, 'quick,' and he sort of held his arms out, almost pleading, and then before I knew where I was I was sort of on the bed and he was tearing at me, very excited and sort of panting, 'Oh, God, oh, God.' His beard was very rough and when he pressed his mouth on to mine I expected to get all the beer and drink he'd had the night before, but his breath was quite sweet, only tasting just a bit of coffee to make a sort of bitter taste. 'In,' he sort of panted, 'get into bed, just for a minute.'

There wasn't time, and I told him so. Howard was in the bath and I could hear the water lapping and plopping as he moved in it, and then the tap on again for more hot water, and he was singing a song very tunelessly, an oldie that somebody had made a record of and was very popular among the teenagers who thought it was a newie:

> 'Waking and sleeping it's always the same,
> Waking and sleeping I whisper your name.
> Give me your lips,
> Give me your heart as well.'

It was a bit weird hearing Howard singing that. Oh, Howard was very nice to have in bed, but he was very gentle all the time, and there was something in me that didn't want this gentleness. And the poet Redvers Glass was not gentle, not a bit, but he went on as though he'd willingly die afterwards if he could just have me now. But I got away from him, I had to, panting a lot myself, putting myself right. It was amazing what he'd managed to do even in that short space of time, but I couldn't have that, any of it, it wasn't right. After all, I hardly knew him at all, I'd only met him the night before. So I said, 'No, no, no,' and took up the tray with the coffee on it, and Redvers Glass turned on his side and groaned as though he was dying.

I got downstairs just in time, because Howard was out of the bath, he was always a quick bather, and in no time at all he'd clicked open the door and was downstairs himself with a towel round him and saying he'd bought new razor-blades yesterday and they must be in the same paper bag as I had the feather finish in that I'd bought, as well as the mascara, and he knew that was downstairs on the sideboard, and that whole business was a very near thing.

Redvers Glass came downstairs yawning, not having shaved, and his hair not combed very well. But you could see he was an attractive man. That's a funny thing, about attractiveness. It's not a matter of handsomeness or a good figure or even a good brain. There was just something about Redvers Glass that seemed to bring out something in me. I looked at them both, him and my Howard, and I knew I loved Howard deeply and dearly, but there was something about Redvers Glass. Howard said:

'What train will you be catching?'

'Train?' said Redvers Glass, surprised. And then he yawned. 'I'm catching no train. I'm staying here in Bradcaster. I rather like the look of Bradcaster.' Then he said:

'Bradcaster, O Bradcaster,
There's holy peace and quiet there.'

'Where will you stay?' asked Howard. 'I take it you've tried all the hotels and they wouldn't take you and that's why you got drunk.'

'Oh, no,' said Redvers Glass, 'that wasn't it at all. I booked in at one place and then I went to have a drink, and I met a very nice sort of Jamaican and we got talking and we went the rounds of the pubs, and some very nice pubs there are, too. But I couldn't remember which hotel I'd booked in at, and it seems that I must have fallen down near that Swinging place, and I do believe that's where I booked in, but I fell down, I think, and after that I only sort of remember being carried.'

'You didn't have any luggage,' said Howard.

'Oh, yes,' Redvers Glass said, 'in the left luggage at the station. One bag. A big one.' And he winked at me in a very serious sort of way.

'Well,' said Howard, 'you'd better be on your way then, hadn't you?'

'I'm disappointed in you,' said Redvers Glass in a sulky sort of way. 'Money you'll give, yes, but no other sort of help, it would seem. Hospitality is better than money. I ask you, I ask you, is it conceivable that I could do this long poem in a hotel bedroom?'

'I don't see why not,' said Howard. I couldn't help it, I could feel these giggles coming on again. I don't know what it was, but there was something about Redvers Glass that made me feel sort of warm and humorous, especially with Howard being so stern about it all.

'You try it, that's all,' said Redvers Glass, just as stern. 'I have no home. The man I was sharing this flat with in Pimlico got married, imagine that, so out poor Glass has to go. And they won't have me in the ancestral mansion of Sir Percival Glass, knight.' He held out his arms, more or less as he'd done to me upstairs in bed, and I went a bit hot and cold. 'Sir Percy does not believe in the arts,' he said, 'except the very useful ones. His son has been a big disappointment to him. And so where can I turn? Only to my patron. My patron needn't think he can regard the giving of money as the end of his obligations. I want to stay here in that room upstairs and work down here at this table.'

'Do you think I'm crackers?' said Howard.

· 'No,' said Redvers Glass. 'I think you're generous, that's what I think. I want a home.' And, believe it or not, he went down on his knees.

'Get up,' said Howard, very gruffly. Then he thought, while Redvers Glass still stayed on his knees winking at me. 'Sir Percival Glass,' said Howard after a bit. 'Born 1899, married Penelope, only daughter of Richard Barker, 1932, one son, two daughters. Glass's Paper Products, old-established family firm. Knighted for political services, 1956 –'

'How do you know all that?' said Redvers Glass, amazed, getting up from the floor.

'It's his photographic memory,' I said. Howard said:

'I was looking up something else in the library. All that Glass stuff just sort of got caught.'

'Well, you can see, can't you?' said Redvers Glass, excited. 'You can see that a man like that would have no time for a son like me.'

'I don't see why not,' said Howard. And then he said, as though he'd given this some thought, 'I tell you what I'll do with you. She and I,' he said, sort of jerking a bit rudely in my direction, 'are going off for a bit of a holiday. To New York and the Caribbean and so on.' He said it without much joy really. 'You can look after the place while we're gone. We'll be back in time for her birthday.'

'Who's *her*?' I said. 'The cat's mother?'

Howard said nothing to that. He said to Redvers Glass, 'You,' sternly, 'are a poet, which is the supreme and most memorable sort of writer there is.' He said it without much joy, like that about New York and the Caribbean.

'Well,' he said, 'I have a bit of a job for you. We, that is to say, she and I, will be going off in four days' time.'

'As soon as that?' I cried out.

'We'll be a week in London,' said Howard, 'staying at Claridge's or the Ritz or some such place before flying off from London Airport. So,' he said to Redvers Glass, 'you can move in here the day we go. I'm paying the rent in advance,' said Howard, 'so you'll have no worries there. Is that all right with you?'

'How long will you be away?' said Redvers Glass.

'Till January 20th,' said Howard. 'We'll be back on that day. And there's this job you can do for me, you being a poet.' He looked at me and said, 'Perhaps you'd better get out, love, and carry on with your shopping.'

'What's all this about?' I asked, a bit cross.

'Nothing much,' he said, in a secretive sort of a way. 'Just a little something that has to be arranged. I was going to do it, but why keep a dog and bark yourself?'

'I've got to pick up my mink,' I said. 'They had to make some alterations to it.'

'You do that,' said Howard, still looking at Redvers Glass. 'You go and see about the milk, I mean mink.' Money had become no object. So, mystified, I got ready to go out. And while I was up in the bedroom, getting ready, Redvers Glass suddenly appeared, having pretended to want to relieve himself, and with the noise of the lavatory flush drowning him, he put his arms round me. 'I'll be at the Swinging whatsit,' he whispered. 'I don't know what room, I've forgotten. Ask for me at the desk, ask for me.' And, like a fool from some points of view, I said yes.

## 15

WAS I BEING a fool or mad or wicked or what? Was it this new way of life that Howard had chosen for us that was causing me to say yes and really intend to meet him at the Swinging Lamp? I just don't know. It's not usual to want to go and meet a man you only met for the first time the day before and, what's more, want to be made love to by him, specially when you still love your husband. Anyway, I got the bus (fancy, with all our money I still got the bus, chiefly because it was a nuisance phoning up for a taxi from a box, but I certainly would pick up a taxi in town near the Town Hall and come home in that) and went into town to this furrier's, Einstein's, which is a very famous name in things other than furs but I can't think what, and there was my lovely mink all ready for me, there having been a bit of an alteration that had to be made to the collar. I'd already paid for it, of course, and the cheque had gone through the bank or whatever had to be done to it, and everybody was all smiles and bows at the furrier's. That's one thing I love about the Jews, their politeness and attentiveness and their real desire to sell you something, not like the rest of the people in England. To give you an example of the rest of the shop-people in Bradcaster, I went to one big store to buy three dozen nylons, and the girl just couldn't care less about it and so I said 'Never mind' and walked out, blazing. Anyway, with my mink on and looking the picture of wealth and loveliness, I wondered about going to meet somebody who was only a poet and a bit dirty and scruffy as well, to meet him moreover in his bedroom after only meeting him the day before when, first, he'd wolfed down all the walnut cake and, second, he'd been drunk and had to be put to bed and snored all night. But this was my new life and I could do what I wanted, thanks very much.

I supposed it was a bit early yet to see if Redvers Glass had arrived at this hotel. I decided I would go and have a drink all on my own at the Royal, which had a lovely cocktail bar with soft lights and I knew Agnes who served behind the bar, because once she'd been on the cash registers at the Hastings Road Supermarket. When I walked in with my mink you could see everybody having a good look and I was very proud, though my heart was thudding away for one reason or another. 'Well,' said Agnes, 'blow me down,' which was a saying of hers. She was smart in a platinum blonde beaky kind of way, and as it was only just gone eleven there weren't many in the bar and she could have a really good look and be really envious. 'Well,' she said, 'that's really smashing. Just like the Queen.' And it was, too, and it had cost as much. Still, I didn't pretend to be a great lady, though everything I wore was expensive, except my perfume. I'd bought a very big Schiaparelli Shocking, but to my nose there was less flavour or smell to it than what I always used, which was a reasonable-priced perfume called Juillet, which I pronounced as Juliet. Here I was being a real Juliet, going to meet my Romeo very secretly. I wish they'd let us read that or act it at school, but we were always told that we wouldn't really like Shakespeare or dig it, rather, it was real square, man. Anyway, I ordered a double gin for myself, with very sweet vermouth, and I asked Agnes what she would have, and she had the same. Then I had another, and I got both more calm and confident and at the same time more excited. But I didn't blab anything out, which is always a big temptation, but very dangerous to another woman, even a close friend, mark my words.

Well, it was time for me to go and my knees felt very weak, and Agnes said, 'You look a bit queer, love, you shouldn't drink that very sweet vermouth,' but I said I was all right. I hadn't said anything about what time I'd be back, and after all it was Howard who'd told me to clear out and do some shopping, but I thought if I got back at about one-thirty that would be all right. After all, Howard had had a good big breakfast and, anyway, he had to go out by himself, I remembered, something about arranging foreign currency for this trip abroad with the bank. Why the whole world can't have all the same money, like £ s d or dollars or cents, I don't know. Anyway, Howard had been frowning a lot about foreign money. So he'd be at the bank this morning getting money and traveller's cheques and things. I walked round with my head up, playing it cool as Mr Slessor would say, to the Swinging Lamp, a nice little hotel, and one or two of the rougher element of the town who were not working gave me the old wolf-whistle, but I kept my head well up in the air. I ought to mention that it was a cold misty sort of a day, but I was lovely and warm. Lovely. And warm. Get it?

I felt a bit shy about asking for Mr Glass at the reception desk, but I did, and they didn't look at me strangely, as you might expect. The girl said, 'One moment, madam,' having a good look at my mink, of course, while she said that. Then she rang up to the room and then she said to me, 'What name shall I say?' and I said, in a very high-class voice, 'Miss Glass,' that being an inspiration on the spur of the moment. 'His sister,' I said, just to make it absolutely above board. I had my gloves on and so nobody could tell whether I was engaged, married or what. 'Is he in?' I asked, which he obviously was. 'I'll go straight up if he is.' 'Room No. 142,' said the girl, and she went on with adding up somebody's bill or something, but not before she'd had another really good look at the mink.

Well, as it was on the first floor, I walked up the stairs, and even after the one flight I was panting a bit, but of course that wasn't all to do with climbing stairs. I found the room, No. 142, and knocked a bit timidly. 'Come in,' called Redvers Glass's voice, so I went in.

I'd read once in some woman's paper, *Female*, I think it was, about a poet who just leapt on women, Lord Byron it was, who married his own sister or something, why couldn't they teach us about him at school? Well, this was Redvers Glass, too, him all over. All over me, I should say. He had this mink of mine off and just lying on the floor of this little room of his, and he had his arms round me and his mouth on mine, he was like a madman, he seemed to want me so badly. It was funny, a man from London, where all the girls are smart and sophisticated, and the son of a sir, too, wanting me with a kind of hunger like that. I felt very queer, I can tell you. I'd never known anything like this before. It makes me blush now to tell about all this, the way he had me on that bed and sort of undressed very skilfully without too much tugging and swearing at straps and things. When I say he seemed to be hungry for me I don't mean that he was selfish, the way some men are. He was hungry to make me love him and want him to love me. First of all I felt ashamed and guilty about Howard, but then this that was going on became far more important than any of those feelings. I just wanted him, that was all, and what I wanted he wanted, too. He did everything right without selfishness, but was still sort of wild and very excited about it all and kept saying, 'Oh, God, this is too much, I don't deserve all this,' over and over. They often talk about time standing still, but I always thought it was just a saying and didn't mean anything, but I should have thought days and days or at least hours went by, but it was less than half an hour from start to finish. When it was all over and I felt really relaxed and on top of the world he was gentle and tender and loving then. I noticed that he'd had a shave before I came up to his room, and he smelled of after-shave lotion, a spicy one, different from Howard's. 'When can I see you again?' he asked. But I just didn't know, it was a bit difficult. In some ways it was a good thing Howard and I were going off on this holiday.

After a bit I got dressed and made up carefully and put the mink on and I was ready to get back. 'Call me a taxi,' I said, and he did, ringing up the desk and asking very nicely in this lovely plummy voice of his. And he kissed me gently, which was considerate of him, me just having made up. 'Tomorrow?' he said. I said I'd see. I looked at the lovely oyster watch Howard had bought me and saw it was only twenty to one. I'd be in nice time to heat up a tinned steak and kidney pudding and boil some potatoes and we could have lunch at the usual time.

When I was on my way home in the taxi, Miss Glass, I giggled at that, I remembered that I'd forgotten to ask Red, as I was to call him, what was this secret thing that Howard had asked him to do, something to do with him being a poet and writer or something. Howard wouldn't tell me, I knew that, you could never get round Howard. So I would have to see Red tomorrow to find out what was going on. I've always hated people having secrets.

## 16

BUT I DIDN'T see him next day nor any day after that till the day we left for London, Howard and I smart, me minky, with all this very new and posh pigskin luggage or whatever it was, with the taxi waiting outside the door. It was up to me to see him, really, and get in touch, not the other way round, and he didn't really try to get in touch. That would have been difficult, anyway, because Howard and I were out nearly all the time these last few days, out at night too, eating, Howard hiring a self-drive Bentley, no it wasn't a Bentley it was a silver-grey Merc, whatever that is, because he said the time was over now for me doing the cooking. It was on the day we left for London that Redvers Glass turned up with his bit of luggage, to be, as he put it, a sort of day-and-night-watchman. He turned up late, so Howard said, but we were in plenty of time for the train and what were a few bob as far as the taxi ticking away was concerned? When Red entered our house he gave me a sort of smouldering look and I went again a bit like jelly at the knees and I had trouble in swallowing and I was sure Howard could see a sort of heart-beat in my neck racing away. Howard handed over to Red a big envelope that was sealed and said, 'Right, you get down to that, you should find it fairly interesting, and turn it into a nice poem that can be published in some paper when the time comes, and I'll tell you when the time comes, so that the whole world can know.'

'What is this?' I said. 'What's going on?'

'Never you mind,' said Howard with a kind of very sad grin. He was a queer sort of man altogether, having all the money any man could ever want and yet looking really sad. I didn't have any clue to the sadness, because we'd had none of this talking in his sleep or switching all the lights of the house on for a long time now. Perhaps it was the rich food, I thought, or the more drink we'd been having lately since we got rich ourselves. Red said to me:

'This is like secret sailing-orders, sweetie.' He shouldn't have used that word, not with Howard there, but Howard took no notice, cleaning his nails with a match, instead of using a nail-file which he could afford hundreds of. 'My little assignment,' said Red. 'To turn dross into poetry.' And he turned on me a sort of burning tight-lipped smile so that I felt this wobbliness all over again. Howard said:

'We'd best be going. Right, now, Glass. I've paid the rent in advance, you see, and I think you'll even find a bit of food in the larder, and the milk and papers will go on coming every day, so you'll be all right there. You get on with the writing of your own thing in the mornings and in the afternoons get on with this other job. And in the evenings don't make too much noise, because you're supposed to be nice and quiet in council houses, this not being like Chelsea. Not that it makes all that difference, those buggers next door having an electric guitar going some nights with the volume turned up.' I didn't like this bossiness and this swearing and calling him Glass. Mr Glass, yes. Redvers or Red, yes. But not just the surname, like that. But there was no doing anything with Howard really. But Red just smiled and said all right. And so we went off, but Red very cleverly managed to kiss me on the neck when Howard started going out first with the luggage, the taxi-driver helping him. He whispered, 'You never came. But it's not all over, is it? Send me a card, write to me.' But all I could do was to smile in a sad sort of way.

My feelings were all mixed-up, I suppose. Every night I'd been lying in bed and I'd been sort of haunted by some of the things that had happened in that room at the Swinging Lamp. I find this very hard to explain, but when you're with a man like that he isn't a man any more, he's just a lot of sounds and a smell and a weight on you. I used to think that remembering things was really a matter of your brain, but this time it was parts of the body that kept on remembering. I was now sort of split and I knew it would be very dangerous to let my feelings run away with me, which would mean running away from Howard. But I can well imagine somebody being ready to give up everything for the sake of that particular thing. I mean, there's little enough in this life, really, and you only find it worth living for the odd moments, and if you think you're going to be able to have those odd moments again, then it makes life wonderful and have a meaning. You might have thought it had a meaning before, like I did, but this was something new and it made everything else seem a bit dim, somehow. Anyway, it was really a very good thing we were off on this holiday, from the point of view of not doing something which everybody would think of as silly and wicked, certainly Mum and Pop would, who we'd seen for a short time to say good-bye the day before, and Mum had cried to see us well-dressed and living it up. 'No, my girl,' I had to keep saying to myself, 'don't get silly. He's only a scruffy poet, and there's more in life than that, and he didn't say a word about love, which is what Howard feels for me and I feel for him.' That's what I kept saying to myself. And how handsome Howard looked and what a good man he was. And there was Red, scruffy and drinking a lot, and anyway he'd only been in my life no more than a couple of days. It was an obsession, that was what it was, an obsession, and when I'd remembered that word I felt a lot better.

Not to make too long a story out of it we got to London and got to this very large hotel by the park in the middle of London, by taxi, of course. It's amazing what clothes do for you, really. If I hadn't had my mink I would have felt really small and all out of place walking into that huge entrance hall full of svelte women and cigarry men, with our pigskin luggage being carried in and the commissionaire saluting when Howard handed over a ten-bob note to him. As it was, I saw nobody there with a mink like mine, but I saw plenty having a good look, and I even think I heard somebody say, 'This is her third husband,' as if I was a film star, but they might have been talking about somebody else. I got the shock of my life, no perhaps I didn't knowing Howard, when I found out that we were booked in in a suite that cost *fifty pounds a day*. You just think of that, very carefully, and you'll see how ridiculous having a lot of money really is. Because if people couldn't afford to pay that amount, well, it stands to reason they'd have to charge much less for it. It was a lovely set of rooms, there's no doubt about that, but I'm sure it wasn't worth what we were paying for it. There was concealed lighting and airconditioning and a gorgeous bathroom, also a cocktail cabinet to which Howard had some bottles brought to fill it up. But in the meantime we had to have some champagne and it had to be the right year too, and the waiter bowed very low and said that would be done. And now Howard turned on his happy sort of smile and said:

'Well, girl, I always said, didn't I? I always said that one of these days we'd go as high as it was possible to go, didn't I? Well, here we are.'

'Yes,' I said. 'But what are we going to *do*?' He didn't quite understand what I meant until I explained. What I meant was really so what? There we were, living it up, but what different things were we doing except having somewhere nice to live and nice things to eat and drink? What were we going to *do*? That was what I wanted to know. Howard said:

'Well, tonight we shall have dinner downstairs in the restaurant here, and after that we shall go to the theatre.'

'What to see?' I said.

'It's a play very well noticed in *The Times*,' said Howard in his lofty, Timesy, sort of way. 'Called *One Hand Clapping*. It's a play dealing with the decay and decadence in the world about us, very witty.'

'Called what?'

'*One Hand Clapping*.'

'That's a silly sort of a name,' I said. 'How can you have just one hand clapping? You've got to have two, haven't you? I mean, there'd be no noise, would there, with just one? You've got to have two to make any noise.' Then I clapped my hands together and I had to giggle, because, as it might be in that harem they have to advertise Fry's Turkish

105

Delight on the TV, the door opened and the waiter came in with champagne, as though I'd been some big Eastern lady clapping for the servant to come.

'It's from Zen Buddhism,' said Howard. 'It's something you have to try and imagine.' He gave the waiter five bob and the waiter looked at it as if some bird had done something in his hand, and then he walked out. That shows you, doesn't it? If they'd charged only two pounds for this suite, which was about what it was worth, he'd have been very glad of a tanner. And the champagne tasted very cold and a bit vinegary, but I didn't say anything. I didn't have a chance to say anything, because Howard was still going on, saying, 'It's a way of getting in touch with Reality, you see, proceeding by way of the absurd.' Poor boy, it was the old photographic brain at it again. 'Like imagining thunder with no noise and a bird flying with no body or head or wings. It's supposed to be a way of getting to God.' I didn't much like the sound of this play at all, but Howard knew best.

We had our dinner downstairs in the restaurant of the hotel, and, do you know, I really enjoyed it. It was a nice-looking sort of restaurant, with concealed lights and lovely white napkins and tablecloths, and at some tables things were sort of going up in flames, and there was a strong smell of like Christmas pudding, but Howard said they were cooking things in brandy. I had a lovely piece of fish and afterwards a very nice very cold wobbly sort of pudding. Then there was Green Chartreuse and coffee. I can't remember what Howard had, but it was a big plateful. I felt lovely and warm. Then we got a taxi and we went to this play. I was a bit disappointed with the theatre, because it was very small, and somehow it seemed to me that now we had plenty of money we should only have big things, like some big pantomime in a big theatre, but of course the pantomime season hadn't started yet. There wasn't a cigarry smell in this theatre, either, nor were there boxes, like at the old Bradcaster Empire. But we had the best seats, so Howard said, these being in the front row. When the curtain went up, what should it be but some young people in a very dirty-looking flat, with washing hanging up, and a girl ironing in her underclothes. And that scene didn't change once, it was the same scene from beginning to end of the whole play. What the play was about was about everybody being very unhappy because they'd got their education paid for by the government, or something, and there was no war on for anybody to fight in, or something like that. One of the actors looked very much like Red, dressed like him too, and he kept swearing all the time. That made me start day-dreaming about Red and it made me twitch a bit, so that Howard looked at me in a strange way. He didn't really like the play, you could see that, and I thought the whole thing was horrid. Here we were with a lot of money, and our first night in London as very rich people had to be spent watching people in a dirty little room with washing hung up and kippers forked out on to plates.

I should have been quite happy to be back in our little house in Bradcaster, sitting by the fire watching the TV. But then there was this question of Red and I was very confused. I felt that I'd sort of got on a bus going to a place I didn't know, and the bus wouldn't stop. I didn't know what I wanted. Perhaps what I wanted was things as they were before. But I didn't want that, either. A bit of excitement had come into my life. I almost felt like crying with a sort of grief and hitting out at people, but plenty of that was going on on the stage.

## 17

I SUPPOSE DURING that week in London Howard must have spent and given away easily a good thousand quid, and perhaps a lot more. He got sort of desperate about giving me a good time and kept saying, 'You *are* enjoying this, aren't you, love? *Say* you're enjoying it,' so I had to keep on saying yes. But what really can you do with money after you've got a certain amount? Some of the things in London we went to see, like the National Gallery and the Tower of London and Westminster Abbey, don't cost anything at all. There's a limit to the amount you can eat and drink, and on one occasion that week I was really sick. We'd had dinner somewhere very posh, with a bottle of Burgundy 1952 or 1953, I forget which, but Howard said they were both good years. My dinner had been a very large pork cutlet, more like a joint really, covered with a very thick rich almost black sauce, and with braised celery and potatoes fried like little sticks. It was very nice. But in the middle of the night I started dreaming about being sick, then I woke up and had to dash to the bathroom to really be sick. Howard was very kind and considerate, but he was also worried-sounding, saying, 'Dear oh dear. I *did* want you to have a good time, but I've only made you sick, that's all I've done,' over and over again. 'All right,' I said. 'Forget it.' And I crawled back to bed and didn't have any trouble going back to sleep, being sort of drugged with what we'd had to drink and absolutely dead-beat. In the morning I wasn't awake till ten and I felt lousy, but they brought coffee up and that made me feel a bit better. But this was living it up.

Howard went out that morning on his own, leaving me to

laze around in my beautiful new peignoir, and when he came
back he looked a bit glum, so I said, 'What's the matter?'

'Oh, nothing,' he said. I said:

'Come on, tell us all about it. I can see there's something
gone wrong somewhere. Have you put all the money on a
horse that went down the drain?'

'No,' said Howard. 'I got picked up by the police, that's
all. I went round, you see, this morning, trying to do a bit of
good, and nobody seemed to want a bit of good being done
to them.' He looked very embarrassed and quite hurt. 'I went
round with five-pound notes, giving them to the poor.'

'You did what?' I said.

'Giving five-pound notes to London's poor, an act of mercy
and charity.'

'Oh, no,' I said, and kept on saying it. Then I said, 'But how
can you tell who the poor are?' It was really amazing, some of
the things that Howard could get up to, there was no limit,
just no limit at all. I said, 'There aren't any poor nowadays,
are there? I mean, since the war everybody's become well-off,
haven't they, and isn't that what all the trouble's about? I
mean, like in that play we saw the other night?'

'There must be a lot of people needing money,' said
Howard. 'That stands to reason, the newspapers being full
of advertisements about distressed gentlewomen and refugees
and so on. Well, I don't see why you should have to give your
money to some organisation that swallows up all the money
in salaries for secretaries and so on. It seemed to me it was
best to give money like they did in the old days, personally
like, to them you see in the streets who need it.'

'Oh, Howard,' I said. 'And what did you do?'

'Just that,' said Howard. 'I went through the streets and
gave a five-pound note here and there, and some said I was
barmy and others said I ought to be ashamed giving away
counterfeit money. And then I saw what I thought was a
distressed gentlewoman –'

'What's that?' I said.

'Oh,' said Howard, 'some old lady who's known better
days and has had lots of servants but now hasn't got them
any more and has to do without. You're supposed to be able

109

to tell them by the clothes they wear, very old smart clothes, and by the way they speak, genteel. Anyway, I saw one of these, as I thought, just off a street called Surrey Street, which is by the Embankment, and I went up to her and said here was a little donation and tried to hand over five pounds, but she started screaming she was being assaulted and insulted and so on, and then the police came along and said 'What's all this here?' Then they took me to the station and I tried to explain, and they said 'You'd better watch your step.' Then they asked me where I lived and I said here at this hotel and they thought I was trying to be funny. So one of them rang up to see if there was a Mr Shirley staying here and was told yes. Then they seemed to think I was just a nice mad sort of person but they warned me to stop doing these charitable acts, but they didn't say no when I gave a hundred quid to their benevolent fund, or whatever it's called. It was different after that, with 'Yes, Mr Shirley' and 'Thank you very much, sir,' but I noticed the sergeant holding one of the five-pound notes up to the light to see if it were real. They're a rotten lot,' said Howard in a disgusted sort of way.

Well, it seemed to me that Howard couldn't be trusted out on his own, so I made up my mind not to do anything that would make me sick or incapable of going out with him any more. But now the week was almost at an end, because the day after tomorrow we had to fly to New York and to really begin our holiday. I had a feeling I wasn't going to like it much, but I was in a funny position all round. When I thought of our little home in Bradcaster, I couldn't help seeing Redvers Glass there working at the living-room table and before I knew where I was I was on the rug in front of the fire with him, and that wasn't right at all. I was sort of lost. I supposed the only thing to do was to keep moving and hope that I'd get over it, for it was really only something physical. The money would all be spent or given away, and I'd even be willing to get rid of my mink if we could be sure of getting what I wanted, namely to be back where we were before, me working at the Hastings Road Supermarket and Howard on some job or other, and just the two of us, happy and only well enough off for a bottle of Cyprus sherry in the sideboard. But

I couldn't stop coming back to seeing that things had changed and things always changed and you couldn't stop them, and you just had to push on and push on.

And so we pushed on to the end of our stay at this very posh hotel overlooking one of the London parks. Howard paid his bill in notes, not by a cheque, and it was horrible to see all that money crackling around, so that you got the impression that everybody would get drunk with money if they didn't watch out. There was Howard dishing out notes in crinkles and crackles to waiters and bootboys and porters and everybody, and he even tried to give a pound note to one of the guests, but this guest, who the man at the desk said was Sir Somebody and very well-known, was very humorous and decent about it, saying we all make mistakes, not like that so-called gentlewoman that Howard had been got into trouble by. And so we went in a taxi to what was called the Air Terminal, all our pigskin luggage round us, and Howard was crackling all over like a bit of roast pork, what with dollar bills and traveller's cheques and so on. Off to America, playing it real cool, man. I wished Mr Slessor could have seen me then, Lady Janet Shirley, off to America. Janet Glass. I had to admit to myself that didn't sound so good.

# 18

IT SEEMED TO me more and more funny that the only new and thrilling thing that came out of Howard's getting all this money was Redvers Glass, and he came into my life really because of Howard's giving away money. But, of course, he had to get it before he gave it away. From now on, flying to New York in the middle of the night, I made up my mind to forget him and make up my mind to live with Howard who was, after all, my husband and was doing his utmost and very best to give me the sort of life he thought I wanted. But flying into terrible and bitter cold seemed a queer sort of way of giving me a good time. It was lovely and warm in the plane, of course, and a real new experience for me, flying. It was an American plane, but you could tell that just from the cut of the uniform of the air hostess, very dark and pretty and tall with it, even though she was English and not American. We had American food on the plane, ham sort of cooked in treacle, and ice cream with apple pie, the crust very flaky. And the coffee was very good and I was really enjoying the flight. But then we landed at Idlewild Airport, which was the airport for New York, and it was bitter cold getting off the plane and I felt very homesick. It was a long time waiting for our bags to go through the Customs, and then we went into a very hot bar and had some coffee and then we travelled to New York itself. We both felt very lost, not knowing anybody, and travelling in the bus, looking out of the window, I was a bit surprised to see that New York was not all skyscrapers after all. It was houses, some of them very shabby-looking, and very slummy for a part of the way. I knew that America was a new country, and it seemed queer that they'd got all these slums there already in that short space of time. Then we entered a big tunnel with very dim lights in it and, coming out, we could see the part of New York that has the skyscrapers, Manhattan as it's called. It was a really breathtaking sight, I'll say that for it, with these buildings just towering up into heaven, and even Howard was a bit impressed. His photographic brain knew all about how many storeys there were in these buildings, but he'd never actually seen them before, and there's all the difference in the world between knowing and seeing.

Now we've all seen America on the films and on television, but there's one thing you can't get, and that's the smell. It was a different sort of smell from London. There was a very icy sharp smell in the air and also there was less of a smell of people being dead, somehow. I can't say exactly what I mean, but when you're in any English town you can't help feeling that millions of people are dead and gone there, all through the ages, and their sort of ghosts are floating about and making the place seem a bit depressing and heavy somehow, but here in New York you didn't have that same feeling. Another thing about the difference between films and the real thing is the people themselves. I saw one man on the street clear his throat in a very loud repulsive way, and you don't see that on the films. But the way the people speak is pretty much what you'd expect, though all the people in New York, taxi-drivers and people in shops and so on, are far more familiar than I expected, never saying sir, but always bud and mac and so on. We got into a taxi from the airline place, a taxi with a yellow top, as on the films, and the driver had his name up on a little card. It was Joe Mancowitz, or something like that, and he said, 'Where to?' in a very rough sort of way. So Howard said, 'The Ritz-Astoria-Waldorf,' and Joe Mancowitz said, 'Okay' in a bitter strangled sort of a voice, as if he didn't want to take us there but if he didn't Howard would perhaps torture his wife and send his children's fingers through the post as a warning, sort of. What amazed me about Howard, though it shouldn't have, really, was that he handled this new money, dollars and cents and dimes and nickels, as if he'd been used to it all his life, but I supposed later he must have tried imagining

113

himself paying off New York taxi-drivers a number of times and then let his brain photograph the picture.

The Ritz-Astoria-Waldorf, if I've got all those the right way round, which I may not have, was bigger than the hotel we'd stayed at in London, a real skyscraper. The people at the desk were very brisk and quick, and they didn't say bud and mac but sir. It was just like home to see how many foreigners there were on the hotel staff, all speaking bad foreign English, and the man I took to be the hotel restaurant's head waiter came through to get change or something from the cashier, and he was obviously an Italian because I heard him say something like *porco* or *sporco* and look very angry about something or somebody. We were taken up in a lift and another man was being taken up too, and he took his hat off because a lady was there, that being me. And here was another thing the films didn't show you, that people in the U.S.A. could have pimples and blackheads just like people in England, for this man who took his hat off had some really nasty pimples on his neck. The boy taking us up in the lift took us so high I thought we'd never stop, it was a real journey. But we landed up right high in the clouds, and our suite, which was a bit like the one in London, overlooked the whole of Manhattan, and it really was breathtaking. Manhattan's an island, really, and it can't move outwards, so to speak, so it's got to move up instead. There were all these very tall buildings, you'd wonder how ever they could stay up, and in the distance you could see the Statue of Liberty holding up her torch and with spikes all round her head, because it's a woman. But the boy who brought us up said we ought really to go to Radio City to the observation roof of the R.C.A., sixty-five storeys up, and that was really something. Howard gave him a dollar, and there we were, alone again, in this fabulous suite of rooms. There was a refrigerator and also a TV set, and this I switched on. Although it was still morning there was a programme blasting away, and there were advertisements, so it felt like home, just a bit, reminding me of the ITV. Then it struck me that all this that was surrounding us was The New World, and that was what England was trying to be like, and for some reason or other I felt very sad and started to cry a bit. 'Never mind, honey,' said Howard just like an American, and he put his arms around me. 'I know you feel lonely and homesick, but there are the two of us, after all, and that's all that matters, isn't it?' When he put his arms round me like that and kissed my ear, I felt something I'd never thought I'd be able to feel, not with Howard, and that was sort of *stifled*, sort of suffocated. So I said:

'I'm all right, really.' And then, 'Phew, isn't it hot?' It *was* hot, too, and you couldn't open the windows. And that day I caught a cold, moving from heat into cold and back again, and that didn't seem to me to be healthy.

But New York was quite interesting, and we saw all the things we'd already seen on the films, like Broadway and Harlem and Madison Square, also Fifth Avenue. The difference between the films and the real thing was, as I said, mainly that the real thing had its own smell and that the real thing was more *genuine*, with people spitting and swearing and having pimples and boils, though not more than the people of England. We also ate quite well, though I was sick again, but being sick seemed to help to cure my bit of a cold. Here you were served with far bigger portions of steak and salad and ice cream than in England, but you weren't expected to eat everything up, everybody left things on their plates, so I suppose that all went to the dogs. When I saw JUMBO STEAKS written up outside a café I asked Howard if they were elephant steaks, and a man passing heard that and roared with laughter. That was about the only time anybody said anything to us, if you can call a man laughing at me saying something to us.

On the fourth day I said to Howard, 'We ought to send post-cards to people at home, oughtn't we?' So we bought some in the hotel, and scribbled the usual thing to Mum and Pop and Myrtle and Michael and to Howard's auntie. And then I thought of Red having made himself at home in our house in Bradcaster, and wondered if I ought to write to him. But I thought, 'Better not,' in case Howard suspected anything. Instead I wrote to the girls at the Hastings Road Supermarket, sending each one separately a post-card, even those I didn't like much. After all, I had all the money and all the time in the world.

## 19

I'VE SAID THAT I caught a bit of a cold and that it seemed to get better, but then the next thing that was wrong with me was my stomach, awful griping pains, and these didn't come on when I'd just eaten something but when we were at a cinema on 52nd Street or some such number, I can't be quite sure with so many numbers to remember, not like our dear old bishops and historical battles in Bradcaster. The film was about some great German scientist who blew everybody up during the war and said Heil Hitler and so on, but when the war was over he said he wasn't a Nazi after all and had really only been pretending for the sake of his wife and children and had not really wanted to blow the not-Nazis up but had been made to. And then he said he would teach the Americans how to blow the Russians up and the Americans said O.K. and gave him a medal. I had to leave, though, before the end because of these awful griping pains. Howard called a cab and the driver did us the favour of taking us back to the hotel though he was pretty sour about it. In the hotel I was really bad, writhing in agony, and Howard had a bit of difficulty getting hold of a doctor. When the doctor came he said it was colic and I must have been eating unripe fruit or something, which I couldn't really remember having done. He gave Howard a prescription and then Howard had to pay him in dollars, not like the National Health back home. Still, he was a nice doctor, very bald and shiny, and he spoke in a soft voice, saying, 'Surely, surely,' all the time. Howard went to a drug-store and brought back some sort of gritty white stuff which I had to drink and that seemed to bring the wind up and I felt better but not well enough to get up. Howard sat on my bed and said, in his new American way, 'Honey, honey, you must get well. There's a lot to do and not all that much time.' I said:

'Why do you keep going on about not being much time? We've got all the time in the world, haven't we? Besides, I don't see that about a lot to do. We've done nothing since we got the money, have we? Nothing at all.' Howard said:

'We've got to have everything that money can buy, that's what we've got to do. It's a sort of duty. We've got to prove that we've done everything we can do with money.' And he went on about this, getting excited, but I didn't see his point. I did see that we were booked on a plane to get us back to England just before my birthday, but as far as I was concerned I would have been quite pleased to go back tomorrow. But I saw again that it wouldn't really be going back, not to our old life anyway, not with Redvers Glass there in our living-room. So I said, 'Anything you say, dear. I'm entirely in your hands.' Howard smiled and said:

'That's my girl.'

I got better and found out that, while I was in bed ill, Howard had worked out some sort of plan for our seeing a bit more of America before Christmas, the idea being to be back in New York for Christmas Day, but before that to see what it was like in some other parts of this very big country. So I let myself be led by Howard, as always, and before I knew where I was I was on a plane flying straight into the sunset and then we were in Cleveland, then Detroit, then Chicago, this last place being well-known to me because of a song about it. All these places were near big lakes, and there I was again getting hot and cold by turns. The next thing was we were flying to Salt Lake City, also on a lake which gives it its name, and after that we flew to Los Angeles in California. It was a lot warmer there and it didn't feel a bit like December. Of course, we had to see Hollywood, but it was just ordinary people like you and me, not film stars at all, and the food upset me. What I remember about Los Angeles is the tomatoes there, the biggest I've ever seen, and the tomato slices you got with a salad were like wheels, they were so big. We also flew to San Francisco, where they have the Golden Gate and the beatniks, real ones, and I quite liked it there. You could get Chinese food, just like in England, and there were actually people there in the hotel who'd never been to New York, and they were Americans!

Well, Christmas was coming now, and the idea was that we get back to New York for that. While we were travelling in the plane I closed my eyes and tried to make up my mind about America and I found I couldn't do it. All you remember about any place is the small things, which means a young lad selling newspapers, picking his nose, and a girl crossing a street in Detroit, I think it was, and her stiletto heel coming off and she had to sort of hop across to the other side. Then in a drive-in eating-place in Hollywood (Howard having hired a car for our use while we were there) a man spilt coffee all down his tie and said, 'For Christ's sake.' Then a man who sold me a packet of sanitary towels in a drug-store had very bad teeth, which you wouldn't see on the films. Some of the buildings were very high and very new, but they have those in London now. I got the idea that wherever you went all that would matter would be the people, and they seem to be all pretty much the same. I suppose the only real reason for travelling is to learn that all people are the same. I tell you that now, so you've no need to waste your money on travelling.

New York had been got up very nicely for Christmas, with all the shops decorated and Father Christmases outside the shops on the sidewalks, as they're called, ringing their bells. And there was actually some snow, which I don't think I've ever seen before in England for Christmas. On the TV, which we looked at one evening in our suite (Howard had kept this suite on all the time we were away, really a terrible waste) there was a very good production of Charles Dickens's *A Christmas Carol*, complete with actors speaking in English accents, which they did very well. I began to feel very goose-pimply, being away from home for Christmas like this, but Howard and I did our Christmas shopping separately, as we always did in England, Howard having given me a great roll of dollar-bills, and I bought him a wrist-watch, a lot of after-shaving stuff, and a dressing-gown. These were all beautifully wrapped up, in Christmassy paper and string, and I began to feel that we might have a good Christmas after all, though so far from home. In one of the stores, on Fifth Avenue it was, the girl who served me seemed to speak with an English voice, and I found out she'd only been in America just under a year, having married an American who'd walked out on her for another woman, and though she didn't come from Bradcaster she was near enough, all these thousands of miles away, for she came from Birmingham. We had quite a chat until the woman who seemed to be in charge of the department came up and gave her a sort of warning look.

Christmas morning was full of snow and there were bells ringing but we didn't go to church. We couldn't really, as we were both brought up Church of England, and you couldn't expect a Church of England in America, could you? It's different for Catholics, I suppose. We had a lot of fun with our presents. Howard had bought me fabulous jewellery – ear-rings and necklaces and a string of *real* pearls. Then, when I'd had some what they call Martinis, nearly all gin, I had a good cry about being away from home, and Howard tried to comfort me. It seemed to me, in a queer sort of way, that we were really punishing ourselves for having so much money, and I told Howard so. He said a very funny thing. He said, 'Life is one big punishment, but, thank God, we don't have to bear more than we want.' In the evening we had our Christmas dinner, just like at home, and there was dancing with a cabaret show, streamers and balloons, and for the first time we really got friendly with people. There was an old couple from Springfield, wherever that is, who were on a visit to New York, and it was their first visit, just like us, and funnily enough we knew more about New York than they did. When you come to think of it, though, those West Indian negroes who live in London know more about London than any English person who's just lived in Bradcaster all their lives. Just because you're of a particular nationality doesn't mean you know more of your own country than a foreigner does. That's funny, though. Anyway, this old couple, Mr and Mrs Murdoch, he being in what he called real estate, made us feel more at home in America than we'd felt all the time, and we were soon laughing and joking with them. We laughed and joked with some young people too, everybody being a bit tight, and I danced with a fair number of quite good-looking young men. Later in the evening Howard and I did some rock 'n' roll, and this soon became an exhibition, because we used to be really good, as I said, and people got off the floor just to watch us, clapping heartily when we'd finished. It was a really good time.

And so, Christmas not having been anywhere near so lonely or strange as I'd expected, we got ready to leave America and fly to the warmth which Howard said was all waiting for us in the West Indies. These West Indies had always seemed a bit vague to me, and I'd never even been quite sure where they were. But I had a look at a map on the plane travelling south, and I was really astonished to see where they were and how many of them there were. Cuba, for instance. I'd always thought Cuba was in Africa. I know that's terribly ignorant and I ought to feel downright ashamed, but I'd never been taught much geography at school. I'd heard of Castro, who runs Cuba, but I'd always thought he was a white man with a beard who'd taken over running this part of Africa, and that's why there was so much trouble in Africa. I must have got him mixed up with Mr Bobumba, or whatever his name was, who was one minute running this other part of Africa and then the next minute in prison, then out of prison again and back to ruling, and everybody cheering all the time. I was very ignorant, but because I was attractive that had never seemed to matter. I said to Howard on the plane, 'When we get back home I'm going to evening classes.' Howard said, 'Too late, too late,' and I knew he was right. I'd missed my chances of learning, really. But it wasn't my fault, was it?

We spent a couple of days in Miami, which is in Florida and still America, and it was really wonderful having all that sunshine and cool drinks clinking with ice and me in various glamorous bikinis reclining on the golden sands being admired by young men with very big muscles. But Howard looked as good as any of them, though he was slighter and had done nothing really about building himself up a big body. And then I thought of Red, who really looked nothing undressed, all pale and flabby, but I still found my heart turning over thinking about him. It wasn't what he was, it was what he could do. Sometimes it's no fun being a woman.

Well, I'm not going to make too much of an account of it, for reading about other people's enjoyment is not much fun, really, and we really did absolutely nothing on the rest of our holiday except spend money. We were in the Bahamas in a posh hotel just lazing about, getting very brown, and the memory I seem to carry from it is the sound of ice in a long drink made out of rum. We paid a visit to Jamaica, and there we heard real calypsos sung and bands with all the instruments made out of old petrol cans. Sometimes I would just catch a glimpse of myself in a shop window when I went shopping, and wonder if that could really be me. I would see a glamorous sunburnt blonde in white linen with dark glasses on, like somebody out of a film. That was me, and it was very hard to believe. I loved the sun and the bathing, and I even went surf-riding, and there were rich-looking and rich-smelling people around, it made you wonder where they got the money from, but I wasn't sorry when January 18th came and it was time for us to fly back to cold England and dirty Bradcaster and get on with this story I'm trying to tell.

## 20

I MUST BE very very careful telling this part of the story, for it's not easy to tell, and my mind gets very confused still when I try to think about it. I remember the dates quite well, though, and those sort of show me that what happened really did happen and you could write it down in a diary, with dates, if you kept a diary. We left Kingston in Jamaica the morning of January 18th, and we were in London the following morning, or rather the middle of the night. I was dead beat and wanted to stay in bed all the next day, which was the 20th, but felt more rested by the afternoon. This was the posh hotel we'd been in before, by the way. We left London on the 20th, my birthday being the next day, and were actually back in Bradcaster, looking very brown and rich so that I felt a bit ashamed, in the evening. Then we got a taxi at the station and I began to feel wobbly, because Redvers Glass was supposed to be in our house. It was always possible that he was unreliable and had just gone, leaving dishes unwashed in the sink, but he'd got this job to do for Howard, whatever it was, and perhaps Howard was going to give him more money when he'd finished the job. I could actually feel my heart beating in my throat as the taxi turned into our street, and there was the house looking like it had always looked, with the TV aerial quite safe on the roof and even smoke coming from the chimney, which meant there was somebody there, and that would be Red. Howard got the driver to carry our bags up to the front door and he paid the driver and gave him a good tip. Then he opened the door and we walked in. The hall looked quite clean and tidy and I was quite surprised. There was the noise of talk coming from the living-room, and then the kitchen door suddenly opened and a young man with a beard came out. It seemed as though he'd been making toffee, to judge from the smell. When he saw us he looked a bit surprised, but then he said, 'Oh. You must be the ones,' which seemed a silly thing to say. Then he darted into the front room, not the living-room but the front room, and we could see there were other people in there, but this young bearded man closed the door quickly. 'What's going on?' said Howard, very grim, and I followed him into the living-room. There was Red, and my heart still beat fast, seeing him, though he looked uglier than before, and he was sitting at one end of the table, writing. At the other there was another young man with a typewriter, and he had very dark rings under his eyes, which I saw when he turned to look at us coming in. 'Well,' said Howard. 'What is all this, a colony or something?'

'Just the right word,' said Redvers Glass, getting up and looking very cheerful. 'A colony. So you're back. Well, I must say you both look very well. But cold, yes, cold. Do sit down by the fire and get warm.' He spoke as if it was his house and not ours and I had this feeling that I wanted to giggle.

'Who are these people?' said Howard. 'I don't recall inviting any of these people to come and stay in my house. Come on, who are they?' The young man with the typewriter said nothing, he just stared, but Red said:

'This is Higgins the provincial novelist. And in the other room, which is a sort of studio, you have Bartram the provincial painter, complete with model.'

'Nude?' I couldn't help saying.

'You look really well and very very beautiful,' said Red to me. 'Your holiday seems to have done you all the good in the world.' And then he said, 'Yes, nude,' and smiled very sweetly with his lips closed. To Howard he said, 'We've been trying to found a sort of provincial artists' colony. Upstairs there's poor young Crosby, also a writer, who's sick most of the time. We said it was better if he could be near the bathroom, so he's actually *in* the bathroom, you see, working there. He writes essays, you know.'

'I don't know,' said Howard. 'And I don't want to know. And now you've all got to get out.'

'But you commissioned me,' said Red. He held up a lot of sheets of paper. 'You commissioned me to write this gloomy poem. It's finished, dead on schedule, but it hasn't been typed out yet.' He waved these sheets of paper, making them rustle.

'Ah'd lark ter say,' said the young man with the typewriter, speaking with a very common accent, 'that it's bin a grairt elp, avin this plairce ter wark in.'

'I'm very glad,' said Howard, sarcastic, 'and now do me the favour of getting out. You knew we were coming back today,' he told Red, 'so I can't understand why your bags aren't packed and you're not ready to go.'

'Only a minute's job,' said Red. 'We none of us have very many possessions.' Howard turned to me with a face like thunder and said:

'Go and turf those people out of the front room.'

'That's not my job,' I said, 'is it? I mean, I'm not head of the household, am I?'

'Nudes in my front room,' said Howard. And then I saw that he was probably shy. So I went, giggling still a bit to myself, to see what I could do. And in the front room this bearded young man was sitting in front of the electric fire, both bars on, eating what looked like warm home-made toffee, and next to him was a very dark untidy girl with all her clothes on, also eating toffee. On the floor lay another young man, flat on his back, his hands behind his head, smoking, looking up at the ceiling as if he was looking up at the clouds. When I came in he rolled his head round to look at me, still on the floor, and his voice came from the floor, saying, 'Who are you?'

'I live here,' I said. 'This is my house. You're all to get out right away.' In the corner I saw a sort of easel with a picture on it, half-finished I supposed it to be, though it didn't look much like the sort of picture I like. It was a modern picture, I supposed it to be.

'Oh, dear,' said the young bearded one, with his mouth full of toffee and licking his fingers. 'Just when we were settling down nicely, too. Ah, well.' And he got up from the couch, which was where he was sitting with this girl, and started to yawn and stretch. As for this girl, she just looked at me in a very intense sort of way, sort of brooding. She didn't seem to me to be very bright. I heard a loud noise, shouting and a bit of thumping, coming from the living-room, so I went back there. Howard and Red and the other man were having some sort of argument, Howard shouting, 'I don't want the outside world any longer, so get out, the lot of you, before I kill you.' Then he picked up the typewriter of this other man, Higgins I think Red said his name was, and tried to sort of shoo them out of the room, using the typewriter, which was a portable one, as a sort of weapon. Then there was a sort of tussle for this typewriter, the Higgins man saying, 'That's marn, that is, let go, yer bustard,' and Red was sort of on to both of them, saying, 'Come on, take it easy, there's no need to be that way, is there?' Then there was sort of a bit of tumbling, and the typewriter fell on the floor and you could see that would do it no good. The Higgins man started to cry and curse, and got down on his knees to his typewriter as though it was a pet animal that had got hurt. Then this Higgins man got up in a great rage and planted a big kick at the TV screen, but for some reason or other it didn't break. But this time I was annoyed, seeing a stranger take liberties like that in our house, and I slapped Higgins on the face. Then Higgins called me a name he shouldn't have used and then Howard jumped on to him and had him on the floor and started to punch away at him. By this time the people from the next room had come in to see what was going on, but Red called to them, 'Out, out, quick,' and they just vanished, but not before I'd made a run at the little black-haired model or whatever she was and pulled at her hair for her. She made a big scream at that but then just ran away. Howard had this Higgins whimpering on the floor, lying there on his stomach, calling Howard a bloody bustard. Red said:

'That was a dirty and swinish thing to do.'

'I'm sick of the lot of you,' said Howard. 'So don't you start telling me what's dirty and swinish and what isn't. All I want from you is to see you out through that front door a bit sharpish.' He was panting all the time he was saying this, by the way. 'Never mind about getting that thing typed. It'll be all right as it is. Thank you very much for doing it.' Howard didn't say that as though he really meant it. 'I suppose you'll want some more money, a sort of fee.' And Howard pulled pound notes and dollar bills out of his pockets, a real lot of them, and put them all on the table. This man Higgins, who'd got up from the floor, stood looking at them sort of awe-struck. He said:

'You brork mah tarprarter, yer bustard.' So Howard said:

'All right, buy yourself a new one,' and put down on the table a lot of five-pound notes. 'Only get out, that's all I ask. Leave me and my wife alone.'

'Oh, Howard,' I said, seeing all this money scooped up by these two. And I looked at Red and Red looked at me, sort of understanding and sympathetic. Then Red gave me what I could only think of as a sort of warning look, and I didn't understand that at all. Red said:

'Right. I'll just go up and pack my few things and Higgins here will too.'

'I'll go up,' I said, 'to see that everything's all right up there. The beds have got to be changed, I suppose.'

'Yer needn't,' said Higgins in a sneering sort of way. 'Yer can chairnge beds when wiv gone. Am not going to be watched over while am packin to see ah dawn't pinch owt.'

'Oh, idiot,' said Red, almost kicking Higgins.

I followed them upstairs, and, really, things were in a bit of a mess. Red only had time to whisper to me, 'Come with me now. You'd better get out. I don't trust the man one little bit. He's mad, that's what he is.'

'Who, Howard?' I whispered back. 'Oh, nonsense.' Then Howard was coming upstairs to the bathroom and in the bathroom another bit of a row started, because there was this other man Crosby actually sitting naked in the bath, which was full of hot water, writing on a sort of board he had spread across the bath. I poked my head round the door and that's what I saw. So there was a bit more trouble, but

126

finally Howard got everybody out, Red still trying to give me these queer warnings of his, but I still couldn't understand. The house was in a bit of a mess, but there were no signs of wild parties or anything like that. It was just that the place needed a real good clean and the sheets were filthy. I said to Howard:

'I'll have to give the house a real going-over tomorrow.'

'Tomorrow,' said Howard, 'is your birthday. You're to do no work on your birthday. You're to do no work ever again, for that matter.'

'I'd almost forgotten,' I said, as we changed the sheets on our bed, in which three people seemed to have been sleeping. 'What are you going to give me for my birthday?' I didn't really mean that, for I didn't want anything. But Howard said:

'The finest present in the world. You just see.' And he smiled ever so lovingly.

## 21

FUNNILY ENOUGH THE kitchen was quite clean, except for a couple of saucepans that were burnt and the nylon pan cleaner was all tangled up with bits of stuff and couldn't be used again. The larder was not empty, as I'd expected, but had tins in it that I was sure I'd never bought, things like Beef Curry with Rice and Creamed Rice Pudding, as though somebody staying in our house had been very fond of rice. Then on the little side-table in the kitchen, the one by the wall under the pan-shelves, I saw bills from the grocer, and I saw that they'd been ordering things in our name and hadn't paid for them yet. They wouldn't now, either. That was a dirty trick, I thought. I was glad, though, in a way, because it helped me to turn against Redvers Glass, and I needed to do that, being home again with Howard and prepared to live a decent quiet life, having seen a bit of the world and not been all that taken with it. And tomorrow was my birthday, too. I remembered the birthdays I'd had before with Howard and how sweet he'd been, never forgetting, always buying me something that showed care and thought, even when we didn't have much money. And now he said he was going to give me the finest present in the world. I must really try, I thought, to stop this physical thing. Howard was very sweet, even though he really wasn't all that sexy, at least not in the way that would really thrill a woman so much that she'd almost want to die with the pain and joy of it. But that wasn't everything in life, was it? No, I didn't suppose it was.

Howard was in the front room, tutting and swearing about the state it was left in, what with tubes of paint and so on on the carpet. Then I heard him say, 'Never mind, never mind,' and go into the living-room. They'd got a good fire going in there, I'll say that for them. It was quite a treat for me to cook something for us after these weeks and months of being a big lady, and I made spaghetti on toast, a good English meal after some of the foreign muck we'd had. I also made a nice big pot of tea, very strong. When I'd set the table and brought the food in I said to Howard, 'Well, it's good to be home, isn't it?' But Howard was still scribbling away on a bit of paper and frowning over a list of figures or something, so I had to say, 'Do come on, dear, your tea's getting cold.' So then he came and sat at the table.

'I've been working things out,' said Howard. 'I make it that we've still got about fifty-five thousand pounds.'

'Oh, that's marvellous, isn't it?' I said, forking in some of this spaghetti on toast. I'd had an idea for some time now, but this was the first time I'd said it aloud. I said, 'Why don't we buy our own house instead of living here in a council one? We could get a lovely one, just outside Bradcaster, almost country it is at Shawwell.' But this surprising Howard said:

'We don't need the money any more. We're going to have a really big house and it won't cost a penny.'

'Where?' I said. 'I do wish you'd take me into your confidence more, Howard. Have you won some other prize or something and kept it a secret? I don't think that a husband should have secrets from his wife. You've been keeping too many things from me. There's the business of this thing, whatever it is, that Red's supposed to have been doing for you. If he knows why shouldn't I know?'

'Red?' he said, frowning.

'Oh, Redvers Glass.'

'I see. Well, you'll find out soon enough.' He smiled. 'Tomorrow's you birthday and then there'll be no more secrets. Tomorrow you'll know everything. I mean that. Tomorrow you'll know everything that can be known.'

'You *are* mysterious,' I said. 'There are a few more bits of spaghetti in the pan. Will you have some more?' Because he was eating very hungrily. But he shook his head, his mouth being full. Then I said, 'Well, what are you

129

going to do with the money?' When he'd stopped chewing he said:

'I think I'll send it to the *Daily Window*.'

'Oh, no,' I said. I was really shocked by that, and I just looked at him with my mouth open. 'Don't we get any of it at all? You mean you're just going to give it all away, just like that? You mean we just go back to where we were before and forget all about it?' For, you see, though I would be quite glad to be living a decent ordinary life again, without being a lady bowed down to in posh hotels and so on, I didn't see why we shouldn't have our own house, say, and our own car, and one or two little comforts like that. I was really shocked at the idea of Howard just giving it all away like that. I said, 'You've always said you don't like the *Daily Window*, anyway. You've always said that it's corrupting or something and harmful or whatever it is you say it is. I just don't understand.'

'They don't get it *really*,' said Howard. 'The idea is that they give it away to different charities. Things like the Guide Dogs and the Starving Chinese Children and the Cancer Research Fund and things like that. Then at the same time they could perhaps publish this thing that Redvers Glass wrote. Although it's a bit long, really. Perhaps they could publish bits of it.' And he frowned over the sheets of paper which he took out of his pocket and which I took to be this poem or whatever it was. I got really mad. I said:

'Oh, I'm sick and tired of not knowing what's going on. You don't tell me anything. You don't treat me like a wife and a companion or whatever it is. You just keep things to yourself all the time and not tell me anything. I'm sick and tired. I tell you. Sick and tired.' Then I cried a bit. Howard came to me and said:

'There, there, it's all for the best really, you'll see. I love you, I do love you, I don't want you to be unhappy, but one of us has to be in charge of our lives and it's better that it should be me. There, there.' And he was kissing my tears away and being sweet. 'Come over to the chair there,' he said, 'and sit on my knee.' So he sat down and I sat on his knee and he told me very gently and softly some of his ideas. 'You see,' he said, 'the idea was to see how much you could buy with money. There was a man who said that if we let ourselves worry about the state of the world we'd go mad and what we had to try and do was to live pleasant. Live pleasant, those are his very words. So it seemed to me the best thing we could do was to get some money, once we'd got the opportunity, and then to see how far money could help us to live pleasant. What I wanted to do really was to sort of prove to both of us that there wasn't all that much you could do with money and that business about living pleasant was really a load of nonsense. Because the world's a terrible place and getting worse and worse every day, and no matter how much you try to live pleasant you can't hide the fact that it's a rotten world and not worth living in. Well, we tried, didn't we? We spent as much money as we could in a very short space of time, and what did we get for it? Nothing, really. Food that was all mucked up and waiters sneering at you, and the bigger the tips you gave them the more they sneered. And a bit of travel, but the world's all the same, wherever you go. And a bit of sunshine in winter, but you can get that easy enough if you wait till summer, which is the moral and decent thing to do. And decent clothes and things. You've got to admit that we've had the best of everything.'

'Oh, yes,' I said, because it was true, we had had.

'So really,' said Howard, 'there was nothing else we were missing, except the things that money can't buy.'

'Love,' I said, 'we've had love, lots of love.'

'I didn't mean love,' he said, with a bit of a smile to show that we *had* had love and he was glad of it. 'I meant things like knowledge and philosophy and music. I meant like being true to the great men who've gone before us and not spitting in their poor dead faces as we have been doing. Like that quiz.' I understood just a bit but not all of what he was saying. And it was a very funny thing, which perhaps only a woman can understand and even then not really understand, but I had a very strong desire all of a sudden to have a baby. I had a very powerful desire come sort of into my whole body to have a child of my own. That was very strange, but I said nothing about it to Howard. Howard said, 'It's

131

too late now. There are certain things I know I could never have had, like being able to understand people like Einstein and Bertrand Russell and so on. Like having an education at Oxford or Cambridge. Like being able to really appreciate the great composers, Beethoven and Bach and so on. And books, too. And all I've had is this photographic brain, a sort of mockery, like having a machine fixed inside your skull.' He looked then as if he was going to cry. I said, stroking the back of his head:

'Oh, come on now, love, there's nothing to get sad about. We may not have had much in the way of all those things you said, like education and whatnot, but we've had a good life and we've seen what money can buy and can't buy. And there's a lot in the world that's very good, really. I mean, there's the birds singing and the sunshine and the flowers, isn't there? And there's us and love, isn't there? There's a lot of good things, I'd say. And we're still young and we've got a lot of life in front of us.' And I went on stroking the back of his head. Howard said:

'It's very hard to explain exactly what I mean. What I mean isn't just you and me and getting a bit of fun out of life before we snuff it. What I mean is a sort of betrayal. It's we who've betrayed things. We've betrayed the kind of world these men in the past had in mind, the kind of world they wanted to build. We've let them down, you and me and everybody. Do you understand what I'm getting at?'

'No,' I said, because I didn't.

'Oh, all right,' he said, sort of wearily.

'Let's go to bed,' I said. 'I'll just wash up and then I'll put a hot water bottle in the bed and then we'll go to bed. O.K.?' And I gave him a tight squeeze just so that he'd know what I meant.

All through our holiday we'd had twin beds. This was the first time for it seemed ages since we'd really slept together in a double bed, and there's nothing like a double bed. While we were in the middle of making love there was a terrific banging at the door downstairs. 'Take no notice,' I said. Howard didn't take any notice, either. I could just hear from downstairs the noise of this banging. It was Redvers Glass. He shouted:

'Let me in. Let me talk to you both. Don't do it. Please don't do it. Let me in.' It was a good thing he'd been made to give his key back to Howard, otherwise he might have just barged in and up the stairs and into the bedroom. He was a man completely without shame. Howard and I weren't in a position to do anything about him shouting like that, and by the time we were he'd gone away. He was obviously drunk. The neighbours told him to shut up and he went away.

## 22

HOWARD SEEMED TO be awake a long time before I was, for when I opened my eyes there he was leaning over me, propped up on his elbow, sort of smiling with his eyes, and when I was awake and staring round as you do when you wake up then he gave me a very light kiss on my forehead and said, 'Happy birthday, darling.'

'Oh,' I said. 'Oh.' And I realised it was my birthday. I wasn't old enough to be frightened or sad at birthdays, nowhere near, but it was another year gone and the years were going all the time. Howard said:

'You just lie there and I'll go down and make you a nice cup of tea.' And he got up and put on the lovely dressing-gown I'd bought him for Christmas in New York and went downstairs. He was being very sweet, and I wondered what presents he'd bring me up with the tea. But he'd said it was going to be a big special present or something. When he came up with the tea to wake me up, because I'd dropped off again, he'd brought nothing but the cup of tea and a few birthday cards, one from Mum and Pop, one from Myrtle and one from my auntie in St Leonards in Sussex. She never forgot to send me a card, but she never sent anything in the way of a present. Howard could see I was a bit disappointed about not getting anything from him. After all, it is the thought that counts, despite what they say, and me having practically everything a woman could want was neither here nor there. Anyway, Howard just smiled and said, 'Later on today. This afternoon. Wait. Be patient.' And he said he'd cook the breakfast and call me when it was ready. So I yawned and stretched a bit, hearing the fat spitting downstairs and the cutlery and plates rattling as Howard set

134

the table. I'd better explain that we had an all-night fire in the living-room and that all you had to do in the morning, if you'd made the fire up properly the night before, was to open it up by turning knobs and get rid of the ash in a big tray underneath. I could hear Howard doing this and trying to get breakfast at the same time and that made me grin a bit. When I turned over on my back almost, feeling very lazy, I stretched my arm out of bed and my hand touched some kind of paper or other under the bed. I picked the paper up and looked at it. It was a piece of very bad typewriting and it seemed to be part of a story. Anyway, I read it. It went like this:

'Things weren't going to be like that for me, I can tell you. I'd heard my father tell of the old days down the mine, the sickening conditions, the daily death-risk, the owner's whip. A fine knotted body he'd had on him, striation of man-strength through the in-bitten blue, and he'd glowed with the old virtues, the pay-night's drunk with the boys his only vice, but too much of a ritual to be really that. But things weren't going to be like that for me. The mines had changed hands now. There was the empty eggface of the Coal Board, now, instead of the drooling crafty leer of Lord Muck or Sir Shithouse Turdworthy, there were pithead baths and Prefects and Zodiacs parked near them, but I wasn't going to be taken in by that. I wanted the best, and the best doesn't go to a man with the knotty shoulders of a world's worker, the indelible ink of coaldust skinned over on his back and belly. I wanted the best – clothes, car, woman. I was going to get the –'

It stopped there. That must be that Higgins, I thought, and I saw him quite clearly downstairs yesterday in my mind's eye, crying over his broken typewriter, with Red standing glaring at Howard. Then I wanted Red there in bed with me, really badly, and disliked myself for wanting that. If I'd been a man, I should have called that *lust*. I was glad when I heard Howard call up that breakfast was ready. I got out of bed as though it was haunted, and wrapped myself warm in my new gorgeous furry dressing-gown and put my warm toes into my mink mules. Then I went downstairs, still hoping that Howard might have been kidding and that there would be a lovely present waiting for me on the table. But there wasn't. There was only eggs and bacon, and my egg was a bit over-cooked, not runny at all. Still, he'd done his best, I supposed. I don't think Howard noticed I was feeling a bit hurt, for he was reading the *Daily Window* while he ate. Anyway, just to show Howard, and also because I didn't really have much appetite, I left most of my breakfast and just drank my tea out of the big cup, putting both hands on it and my elbows on the table. Howard said:

'The same old sort of news. Ten thousand people homeless in the floods, but the front page has all this about this teenage pop singer falling off the stage at Doncaster. Just a day like any other day.'

'Why, is there supposed to be something special about today or something?' I said in a sulky sarky way.

'Today's a very special day,' said Howard. 'More special than you think.' He had a sort of boyish smile as though he really had something up his sleeve, so I had to forgive him in my heart, so to speak, but I was still going to act sulky. 'When you get dressed,' said Howard, 'and I get dressed too, then I'll let you into one of the secrets.'

'Which one?'

'The one about the thing that Glass was doing for me.' Well, of course that sort of intrigued me, and I got down to the washing-up, then went upstairs to make the bed and get ready. Howard had a shave and dressed and we were both downstairs again. It felt a bit queer, all this, like having a will read or something, and I was quite excited. We sat down in the living-room before the fire, which was going nicely, and we lit cigarettes, then Howard started smoothing out these sheets of paper. 'It's very good, this, really,' he said, 'though there's some of it I can't understand. Shall I start to read it?' I said all right and settled myself to listen to it. This is what it was:

Not, of course, that either of us thought
We were too good for this world. No such thought
Had ever entered heads lacking in thought.
But shall I say there was a sort of hopelessness, a sort of
Sickness which further living could not cure,

136

Aggravate rather. We started off with those certain loves
Or desires for love which men have, such as,
Being English, a desire to love England.
But we saw England delivered over to the hands of
The sneerers and sniggerers, the thugs and grinners,
England become a feeble-lighted
Moon of America, our very language defiled
And become slick and gum-chewing.
Oh, and the great unearthed and their heads
Kicked about for footballs. We saw nastiness
Proclaimed as though it were rich natural
Cream and the fourth-rater exalted
So long as her tits were big enough. Alas
For England. England is not an England
We would wish to stand and see defiled further –

'That's not right for poetry, if that's what it is,' I said, 'putting that word in.'

'What word?' asked Howard.

'That rude word,' I said. 'You know what word I mean. That's not right at all.' But Howard took no notice and went on reading aloud:

We've all betrayed our past, we've killed the dream
Our fathers held. Look at us now, look at us:
Shuddering waiting for the bomb to burst,
The ultimate, but not with dignity, oh no.
Grinning like apes in pointed shoes and grinning
National Health teeth, clicking our off-beat fingers
To juke-box clichés, waiting
For death to overtake us, rejecting choice
Because choice seems no longer there. But to two at least
Choice shone, a sun, a gleam of Stoic death.
Better to be out of it steak and kidney
Steak meets kidney and asks to dance
KNOCK KNOCK
The band strikes up with a one-er two-er three
It might as well be steak and kidney pie I can always
Boil some potatoes no need for a second
Vegetable
KNOCK KNOCK KNOCK

I woke up with a bit of start then. I must have sort of nodded off while Howard was reading this poem. It seemed to me to be a very boring poem, with no rhymes or rhythm in it either and I must have just dropped off. Then I realised that there was somebody knocking at the door and Howard was on his feet going to see who it was. I heard voices, three altogether, and the other one I knew was Redvers Glass's voice. I went out into the hall to see what was going on, wrapping my cardigan tight round me for there was a cold wind blowing through the hall. Howard was saying:

'This is all absolute nonsense.' And then I could see that Red had brought a policeman with him, the other way round from last time, when a policeman had brought Red, and I saw that it was the same policeman. I called out:

'Bring them in. Let's know what's going on.'

'Oh,' said Howard, turning round to look at me, 'all this is dangerous nonsense. All right, then, come in.' And Red came in, looking very angry and excited, and the policeman followed, looking as if he wondered what was going on. As I did, too.

'Look,' said Red to me, 'you've got to get out of here. It isn't safe. He's trying to kill you.'

'Who is?' I said.

'*He* is. Your husband. He's going to kill you and then he's going to kill himself. I know he is. It's in that poem. I didn't realise that properly till I'd finished it. But now I know it.'

'Why is he going to kill me?' I said, a good deal astonished by all this.

'Never mind. You've got to get out of here.'

'I'm not going to stand this, officer,' said Howard in his very stern voice. 'This man is making a very serious accusation. I've helped this young man with gifts of money and with hospitality, as you well know, yourself having brought him here when he was dead drunk, and I'm not going to have this sort of thing.'

The policeman didn't look a bit happy. 'Everything seems all raaaart ere,' he said. 'Nobody's murderin nobody. You'd best leave, lad, afore thur's a bit of a barney.'

'It's true,' shouted Red. 'It's all in that poem.'

'Oh, a porm,' said the policeman. 'Rart, lad, you'd best

coom back to stairshun wi me. Narce ot strong cupper'll put yer rart as rairn.'

'Honestly, constable,' smiled Howard, 'do I look like the sort of man who's going to murder his wife?' He put his arm round me.

'That's right,' I said. 'Does he look like the sort of man who's going to murder his wife?' I honestly thought that Red was really a bit cracked and I was glad I hadn't got too much mixed up with him. 'Howard's a man,' I said, 'that wouldn't harm a fly. Would you, dear?' And that poem was a real disappointment. If that was the sort of poetry that Mister Redvers Glass wrote, then he was more than just a bit cracked.

'I'm warning you,' said Red. 'I'll be round again. I'm not going to stand by and see murder done. I've still got some decent feelings left.'

'You'd best coom along, lad,' said the policeman. 'We can't ave yer kip coomin ere an meckin a disturbance in folks' ouses.' And he made as to grab Red by his jacket.

'All right,' said Howard. 'I won't prefer a charge or anything.' He couldn't, though, could he, really? 'I just don't want to be disturbed any more, that's all.'

'I don't give a damn,' shouted Redvers Glass. 'There's something fishy going on here, and I don't like it.'

'What tha larks,' said the policeman, getting very familiar now, 'is narther ere ner thur. Coom alonger me.' And he sort of got Red up on his tiptoes and marched him out, and Red was protesting all the time. I said to Howard:

'What did he mean? How did he get this idea you were going to kill me or something?'

'He's a bit of a fool,' said Howard, 'even though he can write poetry.'

'I don't think he can,' I said. 'I couldn't understand anything of it. A lot of nonsense it struck me as being.'

Howard went out to see Redvers Glass being taken down the street, still going on about things. There were quite a few people looking on, too, because this was Saturday and there were plenty of people at home. Then he shut the front door and came back to me. He said:

'You trust me, don't you? In everything?'

'Of course I do,' I said.

'Really and truly?'

'Of course I do,' I said.

'And you do want to be with me? You do want us to be together for ever and ever?'

'Of course I do. I wouldn't even start beginning to believe anything that Redvers Glass says. I trust you and love you.' That's what I really felt. I realised that I'd been silly to want anything to do with Red. A bit of a flirtation's all right, but you mustn't start trying to break up marriage. Marriage is a very serious thing.

'That's all right, then,' said Howard.

## 23

'THAT'S ALL RIGHT, then,' said Howard. 'Now we'll just see to this business of sending a cheque to the *Daily Window* together with a letter and also this poem that Glass wrote.'

'Oh, you are a fool, Howard,' I said.

'Am I? Am I?' Howard said. 'You'll see whether I'm a fool or not.' And he sat down right away at the table and began writing away in his cheque-book. I turned from him in a bit of a huff, and then I thought, 'Ah, well, the Lord giveth and the Lord taketh away,' and 'Easy come, easy go.' Also I had pretty well what I wanted, including my lovely wonderful mink upstairs and my bits of jewellery and so on. The point was that we had far, far more than we'd had even three months ago, and Howard had proved to me that money didn't make for happiness, really. Also I saw in my mind's eye like a film all the stray dogs and the crying kids that Howard was helping in this way, also the sufferers from cancer and rheumatism and so on, screaming in agony, and there was Howard helping them all, being a hero. So I went round the house singing a bit, doing a bit of dusting, and all the tubes of paint and the unfinished picture in the front room I put in our coal bunker. Then I thought about tomorrow's dinner and what should we have. I called in to Howard:

'What shall we have for Sunday dinner?'

'Oh, anything,' he called back. 'Something in a tin or something. I'm not hungry.'

Silly fool, not really listening. 'All right,' I thought, 'as it's my birthday today Howard shall take me out to lunch at the Green Man tomorrow.' He was the one who'd been saying that I was not to do any more cooking and so on. When I went back into the living-room Howard was just licking the big envelope. Then he said, 'There, that's done. Now get your hat and coat on and we're going round to see your mum and dad and also your sister Myrtle.'

'Oh, why, Howard?' I said, Because I didn't much feel like visiting, it being cold and we'd just come back from the heat. Besides, it was my birthday, and if there was to be any visiting people ought really to be coming visiting *me*. But Howard said:

'We've been away a couple of months, and it's only right and fair that we should go and visit your relations and so on. They'll want to see us to tell us how well we're looking and to hear all about our holiday.'

'They'll only be jealous,' I said. But that was typical of Howard, really. He could be awfully considerate when he wanted to be. Then it struck me as funny that he didn't say that we ought to go and see his auntie as well, she still being in hospital, but it *was* rather a long way away and perhaps he'd go and see her on his own sometime. So I put my mink on and out we went and caught a bus and went to see Mum and Pop. They were a bit surprised to see us, but very glad, even though it was Saturday morning and Mum was cleaning up a bit and Pop doing a sort of repair job to the radio. They wanted to hear about everything and were very interested. They were both looking well, too, and they were pleased with the refrigerator that had been bought for them out of Howard's money. They begged us to stay for dinner, saying, at least Mum saying, that it was only a bit of beef stew but we were very welcome. Howard said:

'I'd like nothing in the world better than some of your lovely beef stew. After all the dressed-up tripe we've had on our travels it'll be a real treat.'

'Tripe, did you say?' said Pop, taking his Woodbine out of his mouth. 'You got tripe in them foreign parts, did you?'

'That was only in a manner of speaking,' said Howard. 'Muck I should really have said, because a lot of it was really just a lot of dressed up nonsense, not worth one hundredth part of what we had to pay for it.'

'Oh, Howard,' I said, 'we had some very nice chicken in

that place in Chicago, just off State Street, you remember.'
That seemed very funny and I almost giggled, thinking of me
talking like that, about what we had to eat in Chicago and
so on. Fancy us having been all over America like that.

'You didn't get to Philadelphia, then,' said my dear Pop.
'Aunt Edith's cousin settled there and was said to be doing
very well in politics. It shows you, doesn't it?' It did show
you, in a way, us talking about America as foreign parts and
yet it's really a place where Aunt Edith's cousin (Aunt Edith
was only an aunt, really, by marriage) went and settled. Not
foreign at all. But my opinion is that there's no place that's
foreign any more. Mars is foreign, and Saturn and the moon
and so on, but no place on earth is really foreign. We proved
that, in a way.

Well, we had some of Mum's lovely beef stew for dinner,
and Pop had some canned beer in the fridge, and afterwards
we had ice cream, a family block split up, and it was all
very nice. Then Howard said, 'Now we're going to see how
Myrtle and Michael are getting on.' Pop said:

'Oh, Michael won't be in, this being Saturday afternoon.
He's become a big United supporter lately and they're playing
at home. But Myrtle will very likely be there.'

'A lovely coat,' said Mum, stroking my mink when I put it
on. 'That must have set you back a few hundred.' Poor Mum.
Then Howard shook hands with Pop and kissed Mum very
tenderly and said, 'God bless you both.' He could be very
sweet, as I've said. And off we went to visit our Myrtle.
There was a young lady called Myrtle who had an affair
with a turtle. She always got very mad if you recited that
to her. We had to wait a bit for a bus and it was really cold,
but you don't find taxis cruising around in Bradcaster. But,
waiting for a bus and getting on it, and a good few people
being on it, I could show off the mink better and I saw a
good number give it the old once-over.

Myrtle and Michael lived in a council flat at the top
of a block of flats in Sunnyvale Road, and it was a bit
pathetic really the way Myrtle and Michael had big ideas
about this flat and wanted it to look like something on the
television. There was the one big living-room with a sort of

dining-recess, and they'd got a sort of little bar at one end, with two stools, and these had been made by a carpenter. But on the bar all they had was a few bottles of bitter lemon and some Portuguese Burgundy, so it was rather pathetic. Myrtle had had these sort of square shelves fitted to the walls, very up-to-date, and artificial flowers and creepers on them. When she came to the door she was wearing black ballerina tights and a black sweater but she looked a lot better than she'd looked that time when she'd tried to do herself in, I will say that. She was very surprised to see us, but she said, 'Come in, how very nice,' and she switched off the radiogram they had which had been playing all twanging guitars, very teenage. Howard said:

'We thought we'd come and see you, having been away for some time.'

'Yes,' said Myrtle, 'how very nice. Do sit down. Take off your coat, Jan,' she said to me, and her eyes sort of devoured my mink. When I took it off she put it to herself, cuddling her chin into it and swaying from side to side, fancying herself. 'Gorgeous, isn't it?' she said. 'Oh, you are lucky, our Jan.' That was really sincere, not catty or nasty as Myrtle so often was. But then Howard said:

'You can have it some day, Myrtle.'

'Have what?' said Myrtle. 'This coat?' She looked in sort of wonder at Howard.

'I'll leave it you in my will,' I said, grinning a bit, only joking.

'You do that,' said Howard, serious. 'You make that promise here and now that Myrtle shall have it.'

'Oh,' said Myrtle, 'I'll go before she will, never fear.'

'You nearly went that time,' said Howard. 'They say you get a new lease that way, like the newspapers perhaps reporting you dead by mistake. You'll live longer than Janet, I reckon.'

'Let's not have all this morbid talk,' said Myrtle. 'Have a drink instead. Let me see, let me see, I can offer you bitter lemon or a nice glass of red wine.' Poor Myrtle. What we should have done really was to bring them a bottle of gin or something as a present. But that's the trouble with being rich.

144

If you're rich you sort of forget other people's needs and you sort of imagine that everybody's the same as you and can buy a bottle of gin without turning a hair. But Howard said:

'Thanks very much, Myrtle, but we're not really staying. What we wanted to say was that you and Michael should come to our house to tea tomorrow. That's right, isn't it, Janet?' I just looked at him with my mouth open, because he'd not said anything to me previously about having them to tea. Now I'd have to buy cakes and things on the way home. But I had to say:

'That's right, you're to come to tea. Then we can talk about what sort of a holiday we had. We can tell you all about Hollywood and Broadway and the Bahamas.'

'Thanks very much,' said Myrtle, genteel. 'You seem to have done a lot,' she went on, 'don't you, with just this thousand pounds? I mean, I don't see how you did it, what with this mink coat costing a fabulous amount.'

'I put some money on a horse,' said Howard, then shut his lips tight.

'I thought it must be something like that,' said Myrtle. 'You *are* a sly one, and no mistake.'

'And now we're going,' said Howard, getting up. No sooner had we arrived than we had to leave. Myrtle gave me back my mink, devouring it again with her eyes, and saying, 'Fabulous, oh you are lucky, our kid.'

When we got outside I scolded Howard for giving them this invitation without telling me first and now I had to go and buy ham and tongue and fancy cakes and a big walnut cake or something. 'It's not fair,' I said. 'We're only just back and today's my birthday and I haven't had time nor inclination to check over the larder and properly clean up and that sort of thing.' Howard just smiled and said, 'Never mind, never mind, sweetie.' Sometimes he made me really mad. And when I said we'd better go to Hastings Road to do a bit of shopping if we were going to have a tea-party tomorrow, Howard said:

'Get nothing special. They'll just have to have what's in the house.' And I said, really mad at him:

'Why do you do these things? Why? Why? Why?'

'Oh,' said Howard, 'Myrtle's one of the family, isn't she? She lived with us that time like one of the family, coming and going as she wanted to. She never knocks at the door, does she? She always barges straight in.'

'Oh, you're impossible,' I said. 'I don't know why I married you sometimes.'

'Never mind, sweetie,' he said, hugging my arm under his. 'I'll make everything right, just you wait and see.'

'And where's this special present you promised me?' I said. 'That's another thing. You seem to be making this a queer sort of birthday for me altogether.'

'Any minute now, love,' said Howard, and we were just coming into Cranmer Road. 'Oh,' he said, 'I forgot to post this letter.' And he took out this envelope and then dumped fifty-odd thousand quid into the post-box at the corner, just like that. There were times when I could have hit him. Hard.

## 24

WE GOT BACK home and built the fire up, because it was perishing out, mink or no mink. Then Howard said, 'Sit down.' I was only too ready to sit down, almost on the fire I was so cold. He sat down himself at the other side of of the fire and said, 'Right. Do you trust me in everything?'

'If you mean sending off that cheque –' I said.

'No, no, in *everything*,' said Howard. 'Do you?' He looked sort of hangdog at me, almost begging for affection, and I remembered Howard in the U.S.A. being very efficient with the airports and dollars and cents and so on, and I had to say, 'Of course I do.' And I did, I supposed.

'Good,' said Howard, and it was as though I'd given the right answer in a quiz or something. 'And it's really us together, the two of us against the world, the pair of us going through hell itself together? Is it that?'

'Yes, yes, of course,' I said, and I went over and sat on his knee. Howard sort of stroked me, looking at his wrist-watch. 'I love you,' I said. 'You've really been the only man in my life.' And I kissed his ear.

'You'd rather die with me than live with anybody else?' said Howard.

'Oh, yes,' I said, and then I said, 'But that's only supposing. I don't like all this talk about dying. We're going to live together. We're still young. We've a long way to go.'

'No,' said Howard, very quietly and in a sort of disgusted voice. 'We've come to the end of the line. At least I have. I don't want any more of it. This afternoon I pass out of time. And if we're to be together it follows that you pass out with me. I fixed this day when I won that money. Your birthday, to make it easy to remember. You're going to get your birthday present very soon now. The finest present anyone could have.' I felt myself growing very cold and I tried to get off Howard's knee so that I could have a better look at him, but I hardly seemed able to move. I said:

'Howard, are you feeling all right? You sure you're not sickening for flu or something?' Because this sort of depression sometimes comes with flu, though usually towards the end of it. My voice seemed to be very small when I said what I said. Howard said:

'I feel all right. Physically I'm quite fit. Look at my tongue, see.' He put his tongue out at me and it was as clean as a dog's tongue. 'And I'm mentally all right, too. My brain's very clear. I've had all this worked out for some time now. In about an hour from now we'll either be in a better world or in no world, which amounts to the same thing.'

'Oh, Howard,' I said, 'you *are* morbid.' Because I still couldn't take in what he was saying. But I was off his knee now and was standing on the hearth-rug looking down at him, very worried by all this.

'It's a rotten world, love,' he said. 'We gave it a chance. We fed money into it like it was a big machine and it paid out nothing. And it's collapsing all around us, decaying with rottenness. It won't last much longer if it goes on as it *is* going on. It'll be finished soon.'

'All right,' I said. 'It's a rotten world, you say.' And I sort of put my arms akimbo. 'I've said it before and I'll say it again, that it's not the world but the people that's in it. And you can't change it, you can't do anything about it. So you put up with it, that's what you do. And I put up with it.' All this time I was talking he sat looking up at me, hangdog, with his hands sort of limp. 'And besides,' I said, 'it's not too bad of a world when you come to look at it. It's a better world than when those men with beards were alive.'

'What men?' he said.

'Those men in the quiz, those old writers and suchlike that you won the big money on. It's better than it was then. It's more healthy, for one thing. You don't get these very narrow streets full of smells and disease that you got then. And they

148

didn't take baths in those days. They didn't take a bath from one year's end to the next. Like Queen Elizabeth, I read about her in a woman's magazine, she hardly ever took a bath. What was the smell like, do you think, with her not taking a bath for over a year? A dirty old bitch, that's what she was.'

'You be careful what you're saying,' said Howard, and you could see he was a bit shocked. 'That's high treason, that sort of remark.'

'She's dead,' I said. 'Queen Elizabeth's dead. The First, that is. It's the Second we have now, and there's all the difference in the world between them. Like chalk and cheese, I'd say. This one is sweet and pretty and a good mother and has a lovely smile, and I shouldn't wonder if she has four baths a day, so there.' I found myself really blazing.

'Never mind,' said Howard, shaking his head in a slow weary sort of a way. 'You're off the point, really. The point is that somebody's got to protest against the world as it is, and we're the people who're going to do it.'

'Oh, nonsense,' I said. 'Leave all that protesting to the people who're paid to do it, M.P.'s and suchlike. People who write in the papers and suchlike. Although,' I said, 'there's nothing to stop you writing to the papers if you want to, protesting about things. But what do you want to protest about?'

'Everything,' said Howard, 'everything. The cheapness and the vulgarity and silliness and the brutishness and nastiness of everything and everybody. The *Daily Window* sums it all up, really. We went on taking it and I was made sick reading it, but it became part of our life and it's the *Daily Window* that's getting this money to spend on good causes, you see. It was all there in the *Daily Window*, people from places like Bermondsey and Stoke-on-Trent pretending to be Americans and writing as if they were Americans. I've nothing against Americans, and we've seen them at first-hand for ourselves, but I don't want to see English people turned into second-hand Americans. But it's not just that. It's this spitting in the eye of everything we used to stand for. There was this writer, you see, D.H. Lawrence, and he said that there was this terrible Old England, like an old lion that kids keep poking sticks at through the bars and the lion's roaring away and is all scabby and old.'

'He wrote about Lady Chatterley, that man,' I said, 'if it's the same one you're referring to. A book full of Sex and actually describing these two people doing it. It came out last year in the Penguins.'

'You're off the point,' yelled Howard, shutting me up. 'The point is about the English lion scabby and jeered at and dying because people throw stones at it. We're not going to see it any longer, you and I. You and I are getting out of it while the going's good.'

It was a bit too much like a TV play or film for me to take in still what Howard was driving at. And very slowly it was starting to dawn on me that Howard had perhaps gone a bit crackers, the result of his having this photographic brain so long, and now it was catching up with him, but I still couldn't take it in as though it was real, it was still something on the TV as far as I was concerned. 'All right,' I said, 'we'll go away again and stay out of England a long time if that'll make you feel any better, but like an idiot you've got rid of all our money and we couldn't very well take up jobs abroad, could we, us not knowing foreign languages?'

Howard shook me a bit then. 'You still don't understand,' he said. 'We've got to be sort of witnesses, sort of martyrs. We've got to show the *Daily Window* and the whole world that we're getting out of the world as a sort of protest. Our deaths will sort of show how two decent ordinary people who'd been given every chance that money can give but no other chance, no other chance at all, how two such people felt about the horrible stinking world. Death, girl, death,' he shouted, and the tip of his tongue was between his teeth and I saw that one of the front ones was going, 'that's what I'm talking about, death, lovely death. We're going to die, girl.'

'No,' I said, 'no,' frightened properly now, trying to get away but he gripped my shoulders very tight, 'no, no.'

'Yes,' said Howard, sort of quiet but wild and savage at the same time, 'we're going to die, girl, and within the next hour, too. So you'd better reconcile yourself to that,

150

because we don't want any final nastiness, do we? We want love and tranquillity, which we've always had together. We want calm and peace at the end as at the beginning and in the middle, too.'

'No,' I cried, still trying to get away. 'I don't want to die. Not yet I don't, not for a long time yet. Let me go, let me go, let me go.'

'You said out of your own mouth,' said Howard, 'that the two of us being together was the important thing, and you can't deny that you said it. Well, it's only right that we're together in death as we were in life, isn't it? Right, then we go together and we'd better not be too long about it, either. So we'd better get undressed here by the fire to be warm, and put on our night things and then we'll be comfortable to go to bed and die.'

I managed to pull myself away enough to bang on the wall, for I was scared out of my wits now, and I banged and banged and banged but nobody was interested, and I yelled, 'Help.' Then I remembered it was Saturday and the people next door, the Hodgkinsons, were always out on Saturday afternoon, he to the football and she and the kids to the pictures, so it was no use, and I supposed it would be much the same if I even got as far as the back-door and opened it and yelled blue murder, everybody being out at something or other.

'It's no good struggling or yelling,' said Howard in a very sad disappointed sort of way. 'You've got to go with me, the two of us have got to go together, but I did hope that you'd see my point right away and come quietly, so to speak, without any fuss or bother. So, if you love me as you say you do, please quieten down and remember I'm your husband and head of the house and what I say goes. See?'

'Oh, Howard,' I cried, 'I don't want either of us to die. I want us both to live and be happy together and perhaps to have a baby and live a good life and give the kid a good education and die nicely in our old age.' I was sobbing properly. 'I do love you,' I said, 'and that's why I don't want to part from you, because it said when we got married "Till death do us part" and that'll be the end of everything,

oh, Howard, Howard.' I was sobbing fit to break my heart
and Howard very gently put me down in my chair and knelt
down in front of me but still kept his hands gripping me so
that I shouldn't get away, not trusting me at all.

'Not the end,' he said. 'There's another world, very likely,
and we shall be together in that other world, happy for ever,
the two of us. And if there's no world afterwards we shall be
at peace in the grave, lying together in eternal rest.' This was
really meant to be consoling to me, I supposed, but it only
made me cry worse than ever. 'There, there,' he said. 'These
old writers that I won the quiz money with, they knew all
about it, they all believed in a life after death, a heaven, so
to speak, where loved ones could be happy with each other
for ever and ever.'

'There's hell, too,' I cried, sobbing away. 'There's eternal
fire and torment and doing away with yourself's a terrible
thing and there's this fire and punishment for ever. It's not
fair,' I yelled. 'I don't want that. I don't want to go to hell, I
want to stay alive.' And looking through my tears at the fire
I could see it needed coal on it, daft fool as I was. Howard
smiled very sadly at me as if I was not right in the head, not
wanting to die but wanting to live instead, and he stroked
my hair with one hand, using the other to stop me getting
away. He said:

'What we're going to do is this. We'll bring our pyjamas
down here and get ready for bed, death being really a kind
of sleep when all's said and done, and then you'll go to bed
first and while you're in bed I'll give you your tablets. Then
when you've had your tablets in about twenty minutes you'll
feel very very sleepy, and then you'll just drop off and fade
out, and that'll be the end of everything. And then when
I'm quite sure that you're sleeping away nicely I'll take my
tablets and go to sleep beside you, with my arms round you
perhaps, and that'll be the end of both of us.'

'No,' I said, 'Oh, no, no, no.' And then, being a woman
and a bit curious, even in a position like this, I said, 'What
tablets? What tablets are you talking about?'

Howard, still holding on to me with one hand, put his
other hand in his trousers pocket and pulled out a bottle of

brown like capsules. 'These,' he said. 'Don't you recognise them?' And I did recognise them. I said:

'Those are the ones Myrtle took that time. You pinched them,' I said. 'You had this in mind all the time, didn't you? A real dirty trick, I call it. Those are not your property, anyway. Those are Myrtle's. You can't use those because they're not yours to use.'

'They worked very nicely on Myrtle,' said Howard, 'or would have done if you hadn't interfered. That's why I took them and kept them. They seemed to work very smoothly. If I'd got other tablets they might not have worked the same. That's why I took these and kept them. I reckon if we took about thirty tablets each that should be enough. Myrtle took about twenty.'

'You're not being fair,' I said. 'She's my sister.' I don't know why it seemed to me he was not being fair on Myrtle. Then I said, 'You can't do it, anyway. Not today you can't. You invited Myrtle to tea tomorrow.' I was sort of triumphant. Howard smiled in this sad way and said:

'I knew what I was doing. The front door won't be locked or anything and Myrtle always just walks in as if she's one of the family –'

'So she is,' I said. 'She is one of the family. She's one of my family. So she is.'

'– So she'll walk in tomorrow calling our names and then when she doesn't see us downstairs she'll call upstairs and she won't get any reply, so then she'll come upstairs and then she'll see us both in bed, then she'll say, "Come on, you lazy pair," and then she'll see that we'll never wake up again, and then she'll call the police and the doctor and so on and then it won't be long before we're in our graves and it'll all be over.'

'That's not fair on Myrtle,' I said, 'giving her a shock like that. And who's going to pay for everything? The funeral and the graves and everything else?' I was going on at Howard as if it was two other people who were going to die, and not me and him.

'That's all right,' said Howard. 'There's about five hundred pounds left in the bank to take care of all that. I left it there

153

deliberately. And there'll be no danger of the milk bottles collecting outside and the newspapers on the mat and us two rotting upstairs. No, everything will be taken care of properly. And now,' he said, 'we'd better get ready.'

'I won't do it,' I said. 'I just can't.'

'Look, honey,' he said, 'if you won't take your tablets and die properly like a good girl you know what I'll have to do, don't you? I'll have to do you in myself in some nasty way.'

'Oh, no,' I said. At that moment he really stopped being Howard who I loved. 'No.'

'I haven't got a gun,' he said. 'All there is is a poker or hammer or that heavy pair of pliers I bought. I don't want to do that. It'd look horrible and it'd give me great pain, having to do that to the girl I love. Because I do love you and always will, right to the end of time and the end of eternity, if eternity can be said to have any end. I couldn't bear to leave you behind, for some other man.' So that was it, I thought, selfishness. 'We've got to go together, so let's go sweetly and lovingly, without any trouble.' And he dragged me out of the living-room into the hall and then sort of pulled me upstairs after him. Then he got his pyjamas and my nightdress and our dressing-gowns, all in one hand, holding me with the other, and dragged me downstairs back to the fire. 'You don't realise how cold it is,' he said, 'till you get away from the fire.'

# 25

WHAT COULD I do really except do what he said? I got
undressed in front of the fire and put my nightie on and, like
a daft fool, I kept thinking all the wrong thoughts, seeing
myself lying dead in bed and hoping that I didn't look silly
with my jaw dropped, and putting my hair in a ribbon so
it would be tidy when I was dead and even putting some
lipstick on to make a lovely corpse. You may laugh, if you
like, you people who've never had this experience, but you
wait till you do and see what happens then. As I looked at
my hair in the mirror I said to my hair, 'Good-bye, golden
hair. You'll never be admired again, except by the worms
underground.' I did, and I don't care whether you believe
me or you don't. And another of my thoughts was that my
life was very tidy as far as the actual time was concerned,
because I was dying to the very day twenty-four years after
I was born and there weren't many people about who you
could say that. There were no odd months and weeks and
days, and that gave me some satisfaction, I don't know why.
All the time, of course, I was also trying to work out schemes
for getting away or perhaps knocking Howard on the head,
and Howard, although he wasn't actually holding on to me,
was looking at me very watchfully all the time. When he was
ready and I was ready he came over to me and just looked
at me and smiled, and I said, 'Well, perhaps we'd better go
upstairs.' Howard said:

'All right.' So I made as to go first. Then I dashed into
the hall, yelling like mad, 'Help, help, help!' and tore at the
front door to open it, but it was locked. Howard grabbed
me and said, 'Silly girl, I thought we'd agreed not to have

any trouble and here you are making a fuss all over again,' and pulled me away from the door. 'When you're nicely asleep,' he said, 'I'll come down and unlock that door so we can be found with no trouble by Myrtle and Michael tomorrow. But you're not getting out of this house, that's certain. You're going upstairs to bed to sleep your last and everlasting sleep.' And he pushed me upstairs very roughly, not loving at all. Then I said:

'Oh, oh, I'm going to be sick.' And I sort of staggered on the landing.

'You'll soon be past all sickness,' said Howard, not very sympathetic. 'Soon there'll be no more sickness for you or for me either. And the best place if you're sick is in bed, so go to it.' And he pushed me into the bedroom, very roughly, not like the Howard I'd married. 'Go on,' he said, 'get into it.'

'Oh,' I said, thinking fast, 'give me a few minutes till I feel better.' I got into bed and I'm quite sure that I looked very sick. 'If I feel sick,' I said, 'I won't be able to keep those tablets down, will I? They'll all come up, won't they? They'll all be wasted.' And I made a sort of going-to-be-sick noise. What I needed was time to think, and I was thinking like mad all the time.

'All right,' said Howard. 'I'll just go and get your glass of water so it will be ready for you when you stop feeling sick.' And he went out to the bathroom, which was just across the landing. What I had to do then was to act very quick, so the first thing was to jump out of bed, though I really was feeling sick now and my limbs had turned to pure jelly. I could hear Howard swilling out the glass several times and from where he was I knew he couldn't see me and I thanked God I was in my bare feet. Panting terribly I dashed like mad and was tearing down the stairs and I had a peculiar thought, which was one that I knew I didn't have time to think about and chew over now, and that was that the house was sort of sympathetic towards me, every room in it and every bit of furniture in it was sort of trying to say that they'd help me if they could but they were sort of all tied down by magic and couldn't do a thing. Then, when I was just rushing into the hallway and not knowing which way to turn I heard Howard come out of the bathroom and he was calling, 'Janet, where are you? Where are you, Jan? I don't want any tricks, Jan, I know you're under that bed, come out now, like a sensible girl.' That gave me time again, and I dithered, moaning to myself, my idea being to run and run, but he'd locked the whole house up and there was no good shouting, as I knew, so then it struck me that I'd have to hit poor Howard and knock him out cold and get the police so I had to look for something to hit him with. I'd always been pretty strong, that was one good thing, though we hadn't done much in the way of PT at school, them trying to interest us girls mainly with ballroom dancing. I dashed into the kitchen and looked around like a mad woman, I could sort of see myself with my eyes all staring, to find something to hit him with. And like a daft fool again I remembered that I'd forgotten to buy tea, seeing the tea canister there on the kitchen side-table. There was my stroke of luck, though, now, for on top of the coal-bucket was a hammer used to break up the big pieces and I'd always told Howard not to do that in the kitchen because of the mess, but it made no difference, he went on doing it. And I saw that it seemed a real waste to build up the fire like we had done when we were going to bed to snuff it. It's amazing what thoughts can fly through your mind, it's as though your mind has become a sort of animal like a puppy or kitten playing about on its own, like you could imagine a kitten playing with a bit of string when it had said on the radio that the end of the world was coming in ten minutes' time and everybody to stand by. And this was pretty near the end of the world, wasn't it?

I stood behind the kitchen door with this hammer clutched very tight in my right hand and I could hear Howard coming down the stairs shouting, 'Jan, Jan, honey, don't play the fool, time's getting on.' Don't play the fool, indeed. 'Jan, Jan,' he was calling in the bit of the hallway that's between the living-room door and the cupboard under the stairs where the vac was kept and where the electrical fuses were kept. 'Jan,' he called as he came into the kitchen and I could see him looking a bit bewildered. I remembered seeing on the television a play in which the woman killed her husband by

157

hitting him on a spot just behind the ear. I didn't want to kill Howard, of course, I just wanted to knock him out and stop his nonsense and then get the police and a doctor and so on, but I had to make sure I knocked him out properly. It was just perfect, the way he stood in the kitchen facing towards the electric cooker with his mouth open, wondering where I could have got to, and out I came from behind the door with my hammer in my hand and caught him this beautiful clonk right behind his right ear. He didn't fall down or anything and I was in ghastly fear that now there'd be no second chances and I'd really have had it this time if I didn't do the job properly, so I gave him another real hit and this time he went down. He went down heavy, and I remember thinking that nobody had ever gone down like that in our house before and you could tell these council houses weren't all that well built because the whole house shook, ornaments rattling and ringing and a tea-cup coming off the shelf and cracking all white pieces on the floor beside Howard. It was like little hard flower petals for Howard. I swear by Almighty God I didn't mean to kill him. It was him who wanted to kill himself, but I didn't want to kill him. My idea was to knock him out so as he'd come to his senses again. He'd gone a bit mad, that was it, and it was all tied up with his photographic brain. But there he was on the kitchen floor dead, and there was no blood to be seen, not a drop, but he was dead all right. I could tell he was dead because he'd stopped breathing. The last bit of breathing he'd done was when I hit him the second time and he sort of groaned. He'd stopped breathing and his pulse had stopped, too. I was feeling his pulse all over the place and there was no beating of it at all. I swear by God Almighty that it wasn't my idea to kill him at all. But there he was on the floor, done in by this coal-hammer.

## 26

THE BEST FIRST thing to do, when you've got a dead body and it's your husband's on the kitchen floor and you don't know what to do about it, is to make yourself a good strong cup of tea. So I put the kettle on and got the tea-things down from the shelf, having to step round Howard to do it. I made myself a really strong pot of tea and I opened a tin of evaporated milk to have with it, more like cream than milk. I don't know why I wanted that instead of milk, normally we just had it with tinned fruit salad, but I felt that I deserved a special cup of tea somehow. Then I sat down in the living-room, sipping this tea and wondering what was best to do. I should really get dressed and go for the police, but was daft again and saw this sort of picture of the police in the station with the wireless on listening for the football results and checking their coupons and I saw their faces when the telephone rang or I just walked in saying it was urgent. They wouldn't be pleased at all. Then I thought perhaps I'd better get through to London, Scotland Yard, Whitehall 1212, this being more their line, a dead body in the kitchen, and they were sure not to be checking their coupons. And then I thought that I needed help and somebody to talk this over with, because I could be in a very funny position, I saw that. The thought of this very funny position made my legs go very weak. I only just saw this very funny position now for the first time as I was pouring myself a second cup and I made the cup rattle against the saucer. Murder. Murder. Murder. But he'd been going to murder me and it was only self-defence what I'd done. You only murder your husband when you hate him and I loved Howard, everybody

159

knew that. Or you murder him when you want his money for yourself or else you want to go off with another man. And none of that was true about me. And then I felt really sick when I remembered about Red, Redvers Glass, and me going off in my mink that time to see him in the hotel and saying I was his sister, and that bitch behind the desk having a good long look at my mink and remembering it. Oh dear oh dear oh dear. And yet it was Red who could help me if anybody could. But where would he be now? Would he be in that hotel? He might even be back in London. The police station would know his address perhaps, but it seemed a bit queer going to the police station to ask for that and saying nothing about me having killed Howard and him lying there on the kitchen floor.

What I did when I'd finished my tea and emptied the tea-pot and rinsed the cup and saucer and plate on which I'd had a couple of ginger snaps, was to go upstairs and get dressed again. It seemed a bit queer to me now that when I got undressed to die I'd put my clothes (it was a beige costume I˙was wearing) in the wardrobe very neatly. But that's what I had done and that's what Howard had done too. We were both very neat people really. I put my beige costume on again and tidied myself up and went downstairs. The lights were on in the house now, of course, and the kitchen light shone down very strongly on poor Howard lying in his pyjamas and dressing-gown on the kitchen floor. He was sort of curled up but his eyes were half-open. Poor Howard. Then I remembered that Howard had locked up the house, back and front, and my front-door key – the one that Red had had when he was staying in the house – had been taken from him by Howard when he'd left the house, and I didn't know where either of the two front-door keys were. I had a long search round and it dawned on me at last that if Howard's idea was to open up the front door as soon as I was snoring away in my last sleep the key would perhaps be on him. And so it was. It was in his dressing-gown pocket and he was lying on it. I had to turn his body on to its back to get into that pocket and the body (I couldn't see it as Howard any more) groaned a bit. I could have hit Howard, he'd been so stupid about everything, and now look what a mess he'd got me into. But Howard was somewhere else and there was this big lump of a body, very heavy and difficult to move.

I put my mink on and went out. My idea was to go to the Swinging Lamp first of all to see if Red was there or if he'd left an address or anything, so I walked quickly, it was very cold, towards the bus-stop for town. And then who should I meet walking along very slowly and heavy-footed but this very policeman who'd been to our house twice before and both times with Red. It was under a lamp, the bus-stop, and I'd just reached it when this copper said, in a very proud way, 'I reckon yer've ad noah more trooble, ave yer, missis? With im, I mean. Haw haw haw.'

'Who?' I said. 'What?'

'That pawit chap as was botherin yer. E's bin oop ere again this evenin an I sent im back. Threatened im with chargin im with disturbin the peace, we did. Haw haw.' This policeman was very pleased with himself.

'Where is he?' I asked. 'I've got to find him.' I had to think fast of a reason why I'd got to find him so I said, 'He's got our front-door key.'

'As, as e? Well, we cawn't ave that, missis. Well, ah saw im arf an hour ago gaw inter the Stag an Ounds an av not sin im coom out yet.' The Stag and Hounds was a pub Howard and I never went into because it was a bit rough. But it was a pub I'd have to go into tonight. So I thanked this copper and went off to the Stag and Hounds which was off Shoe Lane. I didn't much fancy going in there but it was very early in the evening and the pub wouldn't long have been open so there wouldn't be many drunks there. So off I went. It wasn't much of a walk, really. And there was the Stag and Hounds with a light shining on its sign-board, this showing a stag's head and one or two dogs barking up at it. I went into the saloon bar and there were three men there drinking light ale and talking in an angry sort of way about the afternoon's football. They turned when I looked in to give me a good long stare so I made a sort of face at them and went out, Red not being there. I went round the corner into the public bar where women were not supposed to go, and there I was very relieved to see Red sitting at a table with a pint in front of him and he was talking very hard to this other one, the one who'd written about the coal-mines and how he wasn't going to have that sort of life, no sir, Higgins was the name I remembered. There were only a couple of young lads playing darts besides Red and Higgins, so I went straight up to Red, whose head was turned away from me with his talking, and I tapped him on the shoulder. He looked surprised and a bit relieved to see me. I said, 'Come with me, I've got something to tell you. It's very urgent.' He said:

'Sit down, have a drink, you look cold.' But I said:

'This can't wait, it's very urgent, we can't talk in here.' And so he excused himself to Higgins, who looked scruffy as hell, if you don't object to the expression, and downed what was left of his pint of beer and came outside with me. And as we walked back towards our house I tried to break it very gently to him what had happened. He hadn't got an overcoat on, and he shivered a bit and he walked a bit too fast for me, but when it had dawned on him what had happened he suddenly stopped and said:

'Good God.'

'Good God nothing,' I said. And then we passed near this copper who went, 'Haw haw, found im, ave yer? I'll be around, missis, never fear.' After that we sort of bounded to our house and I opened the front door and switched on the hall light. I hoped in a way that the body of Howard might have sort of disappeared by magic while I was out, but it was still there on the floor. Red looked a bit pale and kept saying, 'Good God' over and over again. Then he said, 'You'll have to have the police, you'll just have to. And this is what you hit him with, is it?' He was handling this coal-hammer and sort of swinging it in his hand. 'Very nasty, very nasty indeed.' You could see he didn't watch the TV very much, or go to the pictures much either, for he was covering this coal-hammer handle with finger-prints, I'd cleaned mine off, of course, with the tea-towel, which is what you're supposed to do if you kill somebody. I said:

'It's all right you talking about going for the police, but what are the police going to say? They're going to say that we had a quarrel or something and I did him in. They're not going to believe any of that about him wanting to do himself in but do me in first, are they? That stands to reason. And all this is not fair and a lot of trouble's been caused by Howard's silly ideas. Anyway, he's dead and that's what he wanted. To die, that is. Not quite this way, but it's done the job the same as the other way would have done, not that that was my intention. To call the police in is going to cause a lot of trouble.'

'I'd better do it,' said Red, very loud and nervous and still clutching this hammer in his right hand. 'I'd better ask that policeman out there on the road to come in.'

'You'll cop it worse than I will,' I said, 'you mark my words. There you are with that hammer with all your finger-prints on and none of mine, me having done the correct thing.' He dropped the hammer with a clang on the floor and then started wiping his hands all over his pullover. 'And the police already suspicious,' I said, 'and you having written that poem too about dying in a good cause and so on.'

'That's silly,' said Red. 'What cause would I have to do him in? Besides, I've got alibis for earlier on. This is a lot of nonsense, this is, and I'm getting out of here.'

'Alibis nothing,' I said. 'It might be now you killed him, mightn't it? I could go out screaming all about it, couldn't I?' And the silly idiot had still got his finger-prints all over the hammer. 'They couldn't prove it wasn't now he was done in, could they?' Then I went sort of weak. 'Oh, Red,' I said, 'I'm so miserable. I want help.' And, God forgive me, what I wouldn't have minded then was a bit of love, God help the lot of us.

'The truth,' Red was sort of yelling, and there was sweat on his face even though it was so cold, I still had my mink on, it was perishing in that kitchen. 'the truth can't harm the innocent,' he yelled. 'Tell the truth, get the police in and tell them the truth. The truth won't do you any harm, the truth is your only way. The truth.' He sounded like somebody on a street corner with a soap-box selling magazines. But I wasn't wasting my breath now, I was thinking very hard,

163

and while I was thinking and Red was going on about the truth I gave the coal-hammer a bit of a kick and it went straight under the electric cooker, our model not having a warming drawer at the bottom but little legs and there was a bit of space between the oven part of the cooker and the floor. Red didn't see me do that or hear it either, he was going on so about the truth. But I thought to hell with the truth because nobody would believe the truth. The thing was that I'd got to organise things so that there'd be no trouble for me, for I didn't deserve trouble, God knows I'd had enough. In a little while Red calmed down a bit and said:

'Well, I warned everybody, didn't I? I warned the police and everybody about what was going to happen. They should have listened to me, *you* should have listened to me, but nobody would listen to me, they all thought I was mad.'

'The thing is,' I said, 'what's to be done with poor Howard's body?' The funny part was that Howard lying dead there on the floor, I couldn't sort of feel any sorrow or anything and I knew that would come later when this body was out of the way. 'We just can't leave the body lying here,' I said. Red said:

'Leave me out of it, it's nothing to do with me, I don't want anything to do with it or any part of it, I just want to be left out of it.'

By now my brain was working very quickly, very cool, real cool, man, silly old idiot he'd been, and I said:

'Your finger-prints are all over that hammer and you don't know where that hammer is.' He said:

'Where is it, where is it, what have you done with it, where have you hidden it?'

'It's in this kitchen,' I said, 'and while you're looking for it I'll just go out and bring in that copper. Nice that'll be, won't it, you on your knees looking for that hammer and a copper coming in to see this dead body and you all in a dither as you are. Come on,' I said, 'play it real cool.' Stupid of me. Red wasn't all that bright, really, you could see that. He was all right in bed, and that was about all, but I suppose you have to be thankful for small mercies. 'I've got a cheque-book,' I said, 'with all Howard's signatures on it. If I go to the bank on Monday morning I can draw out this fifty-odd thousand quid can't I?'

'How much?' said Red.

I had to tell him again. 'And,' I said, 'the *Daily Window* won't be quick enough with their cheque, will they? They'll be a bit annoyed, but what you've never had you've never missed, and that goes for everybody.'

'I don't like this one little bit,' said Red.

'You will,' I said. 'And there's nothing to feel guilty about, really. Howard didn't want his money and he wanted to die. So there's nothing to feel guilty about.'

'What are you going to do?' asked Red.

'We could go abroad,' I said, 'taking Howard with us. I've got some lovely new luggage. There's a lovely big trunk we never used. Howard can go in that. Before he gets stiff, that is.' I was handling this real cool, that's really the only expression you can think of.

'I don't like this one little bit,' said Red again.

'Oh, come off it,' I said. I'd really taken over now. I was really in charge and I was quite enjoying it. I was only wishing that things could get moving a bit faster, what with tomorrow being Sunday and nowhere open. And then that fool Howard had invited Myrtle and Michael to tea. Well, they shouldn't come. It had been no idea of mine. Tomorrow morning first thing I'd go round and tell them that Howard was taking me out for the day as a kind of day-after-my-birthday treat and they could come to tea some other time. 'Oh, poor stupid Howard,' I kept thinking when later on Red and I were stuffing him into this lovely big pigskin-covered trunk. He went in very nicely, doubled up of course.

## 27

TO DO A fiddle with a passport isn't really all that difficult. It was lucky in a way that Howard and I hadn't travelled on two separate passports. What we'd done was to get one, really Howard's, with our two photographs on the one page, me as wife or *femme*, with this Foreign Office stamp stamped on to both photographs, but with only a very little bit of it on Howard's, just the sort of curve of the kind of oval that has the lion and unicorn inside and FOREIGN OFFICE. So it was no real trouble for Red to get a passport photograph taken (ready while you wait) at Bealby's on the Monday and stick that on Howard's passport on Page 3, first of course having removed Howard's photograph. It was only for crossing the Channel anyway and nobody was going to look too closely, and the description on Page 2 is a bit vague, Red anyway having brownish hair just like Howard, also being the same age and only a bit shorter in height.

I had a bit of trouble at the bank on Monday morning, not really trouble so much as everybody getting into a bit of a flap because I wanted to draw out so much money. But there was Howard's signature and they couldn't get away from it, it was no business of theirs, it was Howard's money and it was now rightfully mine. I had to see the manager and I explained we were going abroad again, and he said he didn't like this at all, really, cashing a big cheque like that, but I said it was no business of his and I'd take full responsibility. He said he hoped I realised the regulations about exporting currency and I told him yes, I knew all about it and then I had a brainwave and said the money was for buying jewellery and Howard had left everything to me in that respect. Well, after this big flap and humming and hah-ing, I got the cash in what was called big denominations and I had it all in one of these pigskin cases. So the *Daily Window* wouldn't get a penny.

I'd write to the council housing committee or whatever it was when I got over to France and say that we didn't want the house any more, my husband and I now going to live abroad, and they could do what they liked with the TV and the furniture and so on, perhaps give it to some old-age pensioner or somebody who needed it. Howard would have liked that. I packed practically everything else, including the coal-hammer in a yellow duster, and Red had Howard's suitcases and also his clothes, which fitted him reasonably well. The idea was that we were going off to Paris for a bit, Red saying he knew Paris well and could speak French well, and then find a villa or something somewhere. Anyway, he was quite efficient himself, getting Continental Trunks on the telephone and booking in, *in French*, in a hotel called the Superbe or something, as Monsieur and Madame Shirley. British Railways made no trouble about collecting the luggage, though they sweated a bit over the trunk with poor Howard in it. That trunk was in the luggage van when we travelled down to Folkestone and it was on board the boat with us when we crossed the Channel, I being very sick.

At Boulogne, in France, the Customs people didn't seem very interested in our luggage, and Red made a joke about the trunk, saying there was a dead body in it, and everybody had a good laugh about that. The dead body of poor Howard was only a few days old and it was very cold weather, being the end of January, but there was still the question of getting rid of it in a way that nobody would be suspicious about, and Red said being in France was not really like being in a foreign country, because there was Interpol nowadays and Scotland Yard all nicely tied up with the Sûreté and so on. So he said we had to be careful.

I loved Paris really, the shops and so on, though it was very damp and cold, and Red got back something of his old spirit and was very loving. He began to see that we had nothing to be guilty about and my conscience was quite clear, there being only the question of this body of poor Howard's. There it was, in this trunk in our hotel bedroom, and sometimes it didn't seem quite decent to be there with Red and Howard, though no longer alive, there too. We thought of all sorts of things, such as setting the hotel on fire, but that didn't seem fair somehow. But one day Red hit on an idea which seemed as if it might work. He said:

'That shop in Rue What's-its-name. Where they have the antiques and things.'

'Yes?'

'They have a Chinese camphorwood chest. A nice big one. Camphor will preserve anything. A lovely smell, too. We'll go and buy that.'

'All right,' I said. So we went to this shop and Red spoke in French to the old man who ran the place. This chest was a nicely carved big box, all covered with dragons, very cleverly done. It was very big, too, as big as my trunk. Poor Howard. Anyway, Red managed to get it for one thousand new francs, which he said wasn't too dear, considering. This chest was brought to our hotel on a lorry and it was much admired by the hotel staff, even those who had to bring it up to our room. Then, when we'd locked the door, we bundled poor Howard's dead body out of my trunk on to the floor. It was looking less and less like Howard now, but it made me feel a bit distressed and sick as we put it into the camphorwood chest. It went in very nicely, and Red was right about the lovely smell of camphor that came off this box. So now the body was all right and we didn't have to hurry too much about finding somewhere more or less permanent to live.

Not to make too long a story of it, and I have tried to keep this whole thing short, you have to admit that, we took a lease for a year on a kind of bungalow in the country, not too far from a place called Montmorillon, which is west of a river called the Vienne. We took all our luggage with us, of course, and the two important parts of our luggage were this chest with Howard's body in it and my pigskin case full of English money of high denomination, as they call it. The chest has been put in a room all by itself, for there are a lot of rooms, none of them with much furniture in them, but of course we can't have this body of Howard's there for ever.

What Red says he's going to do is to start sowing seeds on the big patch of land at the back, and he's going to prop poor old Howard's body up as a scarecrow, saying that the crows will make short work of him. That sounds a bit creepy, but it's only a dead body and Howard's no longer anything to do with it. It's perhaps what Howard himself would have wished, to try and scare blackbirds off from seeds.

It's very hard for me to feel any real sorrow for Howard. I miss him sometimes, especially with Red carrying on a bit, as I think he is, with a woman called Madame Crébillon about seven miles down the road. That's why I've got this coal-hammer still. Because there's a man called Henri Fournier who has something to do with wine and speaks English really very well and says he'd do anything for me. What's sauce for the goose is sauce for the gander. Because now all Red has to do is to say he's sick of the modern world and he wants to leave it, taking me with him, and then the old coal-hammer will come into play, and that won't be murder, it will be self-defence, like with Howard. But what I was going to say was that it's hard to feel any sorrow for Howard really, because he's got what he wanted, except of course that I didn't go with him. Howard was just a handsome machine wanting to die, and Red says that that's what the world is today. If he keeps on saying it I'll know it's time to keep my fingers on that coal-hammer. Not that I really wish anybody any harm, because all I want is to live a nice decent life, getting as much pleasure out of it as I can. That's what we're here for, when all's said and done.

I've finished writing my story now, and that's my story, and whether you believe it or not is your business and not mine. Some people have been saying unkind things about Red and me, about murder and robbery and so on, I don't know where the stories started, perhaps even in the Hastings Road Supermarket, the world being a small place nowadays, but the story I've told you is the story I stick to. And my final words are to those who worry about the modern world and about life and so on. They're not my words really but Pop's words (my father, that is) and they're not so much his words as words he was always quoting from a corporal who said

169

them to him during the Second World War. This corporal was giving them a lesson on the rifle or something, and somebody said, 'How long do you think this war's going to last, Corporal?' And the corporal said, 'What does it matter how long it lasts so long as there's still plenty of beer and fags?' Well, I don't go much for either of those two things, but I see his point. And Howard, by the way, when he was doing his national service, was said by everybody not to be much of a soldier. Let me like a soldier fall. That's just what he didn't say, did he? Poor silly Howard.